CRASH
AND
BURN

SA REILLY

Tellwell Talent
www.tellwell.ca

ISBN
978-1-77370-235-3 (Paperback)
978-1-77370-236-0 (eBook)

DEDICATED TO MASTIN KIPP AND PAT VERDUCCI.
WITHOUT YOU THIS BOOK WOULD BE
NEITHER WRITTEN NOR READABLE.
FROM THE BOTTOM OF MY HEART: THANK YOU.

ACKNOWLEDGEMENTS

Many wonderful people contributed to this book's existence and the conditions that allowed it.

In no particular order, and with a ton of love and immense gratitude:

Jenna, thank you for seeing me. I will forever associate you with crazy ideas, quiet confidence and steadfast belief in ridiculously-sized dreams.

Alicia, thank you for being the best writing buddy anyone could ask for! Only with your drive and support could a non-writer complete an entire novel in 12 days flat. Thank you for the coffee and the laughs, and the die-hard motivation. You are a true role model.

Claire and Greg, thank you for the bed and the dinners while I slaved over drafts 2 through 6. It was grueling and your generosity is the reason I remember it so fondly.

Dad, thank you for gifting me the very laptop I wrote this on. You were 100% right – I definitely needed a MacBook.

The Kerridges, thank you to my wonderful family members who celebrated and supported my acceptance onto the writers' retreat that ultimately changed my life.

Jeff, thank you for lending me your name to use and abuse on a character with as many flaws as you have strengths.

Gillian, thank you for your kindness, support and office (!) as I did battle with the final revision.

Sarah, thank you for being the fastest peer-reviewer in the southern hemisphere!

Trudy, thank you for (just casually) catching the 1-word error that would've completely derailed my favorite part of the book.

Joel, thank you for taking the time to educate me about brake cables.

And to everyone else in my life who inspires and supports me, thank you.

You mean the world to me.

Lay beside me, under wicked skies
Through black of day, dark of night, we share this, paralyze
The door cracks open but there's no sun shining through
Black heart scarring darker still, but
there's no sun shining through

Metallica: 'The Unforgiven II'

CHAPTER ONE

Closing the front door behind him, James dropped his keys into the green ceramic dish on the sideboard and stepped out of his work boots. Digging his fingers into the knots interlaced through his neck and shoulders, he took a few deep breaths and steeled himself for the impending chit-chat. While Novella didn't appear to have any suspicions yet, he didn't want or need any scrutiny. They'd been married for almost four years; in fact, their anniversary was coming up. James glanced at the calendar on the wall of their bedroom, where the date was encircled in a pink heart.

Novella arrived home shortly after him. He heard her call his name as he was stepping out of the shower, and pulled on some old sweats in order to give her the impression that he was done for the day. He needed them to have an early night if she was to be sleeping deeply enough by the time he had to leave. He jogged heavily down the stairs and entered the kitchen where she was unpacking food on the kitchen counter.

"I couldn't be bothered cooking tonight, so I just grabbed some Thai," she said.

"Excellent." He eyed the containers hungrily. "Let's watch a movie or something. I don't have any energy tonight." He tried to look impassive.

Novella fished two plates out of the pantry. "I'll be lucky if I can go a whole movie, to be honest. Pick something short."

Novella was a very petite and feminine creature. She had delicate features and a penchant for pencil skirts that flattered her short but shapely figure. She was a naturally energetic person, and rarely came straight home from work. If she wasn't at the gym, she was at happy hour with her girlfriends (whom James was invariably critical of) or shopping, or visiting family. She reminded him of an old power drill; she needed to be completely drained before the recharge, lest the battery remember and have less capacity the next day.

She had decided to grow out her regular pixie-style hair cut a couple of years ago, and the leftover layers had weathered what was normally quite an awkward stage surprisingly well. Her hair was just past shoulder length and framed her face flatteringly. Her almond eyes were wide-set and her mouth, though small, had a defined cupid's bow that held its position, even when she smiled widely.

But what James liked most about her was her unfailing optimism. Whenever something went wrong, or seemed unfixable, she never panicked. She never flapped, or shouted, or lamented, or blamed. She merely made a cup of tea, broke the problem down, and devised a plan. She firmly believed everything could be figured out with dignity and a total absence of drama.

They didn't have anything especially short, so James chose *Love Actually* because it was Novella's favorite film, but he was too preoccupied with his plans for the evening to follow the plot. After Novella asked him if he understood the joke for the second time, he stopped pretending to watch and put his arms around her. "I'm going up to bed honey. I'll see you when you're done." Planting a kiss on the side of her head, he picked up the plates and took them out to the kitchen. While he rinsed and placed them in the dish rack he could hear her turning off the television and drawing curtains.

She padded into the room looking sleepy. James looked up. "Couldn't last either?"

"No, I'm done. I've already seen it a hundred times anyway."

In the bedroom, Novella changed and climbed into bed. James wrapped himself around her and began stroking her hair.

"That's nice," she said, sleepily.

I know, he thought, willing her to fall asleep quickly. As she settled into a regular breathing pattern, he made a mental list of everything he still needed to find. He would take a change of clothes so that his sweats didn't smell of smoke. He also needed to take his hip flask out of the cabinet downstairs because he didn't want to use petrol this time. He liked to change up the fuels and other little details so that any investigation wouldn't link them together.

James tried rolling away to see if she stirred. No reaction. He lay on his back for a while, staring at the ceiling and listening to her breathing. He always waited at least forty-five minutes to ensure she was in the middle of a sleep cycle before he tried to get out of the bed. He was too hot under the covers in his clothes, but he wouldn't rush the process. This routine had worked well a few times now, and since it wasn't broke, he wouldn't be fixing it.

When the clock struck eleven, he held the blankets down between them to avoid dragging them off her, and carefully eased himself out of the bed. Barefoot, he collected the clothing he needed from the bottom of the closet where he had left them separated and folded, and crept down the stairs. It wasn't a long drive, but he would need to spend a little time scouting the area first to make sure he wasn't likely to be seen by any homeless people frequenting the area. Though their testimony was not reliable, he simply didn't take those kinds of risks.

The driveway sloped downwards, so James was able to release the handbrake and roll out into the street a little way before starting the engine. He kept his foot light on the accelerator and hummed along in first gear for about a block before he felt safe to make any real noise. While the creeping about was necessary, it also added to the excitement.

The drive to the target was always exhilarating. The fear of being stopped for something routine, only to have the cop smell accelerant and search him. The feeling of anticipation, knowing the release was imminent. The trepidation of approaching a new building and scouting for potential witnesses. And the pure thrill of destruction. The heat, the smoke, the catharsis.

•　　•　　•　　•

James pulled into a parking lot and jogged briskly through the park towards the old factory at the end of Smith Street. It had rained earlier, and the wet grass soaked the bottom of his jeans. The sodden denim slapped against his ankles and made them itch. Every time he reached down to scratch the skin, red and white from his impatient nails and the clammy cold, he cursed the seamstress that had hemmed them too short.

"I don't think she factored in the hem when she cut them," Novella had said, holding them up against him, and looking tolerantly at the freshly pressed legs hovering comically high above his shoes.

"Useless," James had replied. "I hope you didn't pay her."

"Of course, I paid her. I didn't know she'd messed it up until now."

Novella had offered to take them back and complain, but he planned to throw away tonight's clothes to avoid having to explain the smell anyway.

"I'll just put them in the charity bin up the road," he'd said dismissively. "I didn't really like the color."

James surveyed the building from a crouched position in the bushes between the factory and the park. The brickwork was cracked and uneven, the windows smeared and damaged with several web-like fractures. It was a small, family-owned factory that produced hand-made, Victorian style furniture. It was popular with those who liked the look of antiques, but couldn't stomach the price of the real thing.

James had decided on this building after the newspaper released the details of the first attempted robbery. The journalist dutifully reported every morsel of information they could find in order to pad out the inconsiderable story, and had mentioned the absence of an alarm. The owner of the factory was an overweight man in his late fifties with a nose like a red avocado and the disenchanted eyes of someone who knows better but lives that way out of spite. He had proudly asserted, "I have lived in this town my whole life and I know everyone worth knowing. Anyone stupid enough to rob me will be found out in a matter of hours. You mark my words."

Languid clouds left over from the storm drifted across the harvest moon, sporadically dimming his view. He tried to shift his weight to the other leg without creating any rustling; a protruding twig jabbed him in the side of the neck and his left arm shot out in fright, snapping the small branch and momentarily upsetting his balance. Teetering precariously on one foot, with his left hand strangling the base of the offending bush, he tried to silence his breathing while he waited for his heart to stop pounding. He peered around nervously, but there was no one in the park. Tear-drop shaped leaves on the feathery bough of the ash tree behind him wavered gently, skimming a breeze he couldn't feel.

The positioning of the factory's spotlights seemed arbitrary and pointless, intermittently illuminating an unclimbable rear fence and the garbage bins. Occasionally, a stray cat would trigger the sensor and freeze, wide-eyed for a few seconds before scuttling back into the shadows.

There was originally a sensor for the main entrance, but several months earlier some diligent, but ultimately unsuccessful, thieves had attempted to divert the light from their bumbling attempts at lock-pickery, by shoving it around with the bristled end of a broom. They had succeeded in cracking the external glass casing and angling the light awkwardly back into the building. Had James inadvertently triggered it, it would have created an interesting spectacle, sending shards of dissected fluorescent bouncing around the inside of the factory, courtesy of all the metal molds inside.

Mentally willing away stray animals, James eased himself out of the bush. The gravel of the factory courtyard crunched beneath his feet as he scuttled, bent over and tense, to the far right side of the entrance. Assuming the sensor had a wide spectrum, he kept his back firm against the wall, and approached the front door one painfully slow step at a time.

James reached into his pocket and pulled out a small tension wrench and a large paperclip. Holding one end of the paperclip in his teeth, he unfolded it half way, and bent the end to a right angle. He inserted the tension wrench into the base of the key hole and pressed gently from side to side, feeling for the tell-tale give. Bracing the wrench in place with his left hand, he inserted the bent end of the paperclip into the top of the keyhole and dragged it out slowly, raking the pins and mentally counting the bumps. He paused to look around, scanning the courtyard anxiously, and tried to discern blurry shapes in the disobedient moonlight.

Confident he was still alone, he reached the paperclip back in, and began pressing each individual pin with the upturned end. As each one clicked up, he increased the pressure on the tension wrench ever so slightly. As the fifth pin gave, the wrench spun to the right and the lock snapped open.

James shoved the tools hastily into his pocket, said a silent thank you to YouTube, and eased the door open, leaving just enough space to allow him to slide through. Inside the factory, the air was thick with dust and damp. Instantly, he could taste the metallic tang of the particulate matter and began breathing through his nose. Brown mould fringed the edges of the louvered windows, shadowing rainwater stains and disappearing behind tool boards. He wrinkled his nose and scanned the shop floor for dry areas and smaller flammable items. He would need to start in the middle, away from the cold, uninsulated walls. His hands were shaking from the chill in the air and the excitement. Nothing else gave him such a glorious mix of energy and anticipation.

This old factory was just like the first factory he burned. He liked industrial buildings because they provided much of their own ammunition, were more or less easy to get into, and practically never ran a nightshift as the noise and their close proximity to residential areas made it impossible to operate after dark. Strolling casually around the workstations with a practiced eye, he methodically collected anything resembling kindling. Logbooks, notes, furniture and wooden-handled tools migrated to a steadily growing pyramid of consumables on a heavy wooden workbench that sat in the center of the factory's workshop between two large machines. The first one was a lathe, the second he didn't recognize.

A dusty old chair, warped and dotted with flecks of various varnishes and coatings, sat friendless in the corner of the room. He collected it in sweeping strides and, swinging it above his head, he brought it down as hard as he could against the side of the bench. It made a terrific cracking noise, and one of the legs snapped off and flew, spinning past his head. He jerked out of the way with an unintentional "Whoa!"

The leg's tinny landing and raspy slide along the dusty concrete floor sounded even louder against the silence that seemed magnified by his outburst. He paused a moment and looked around at the doors and windows. No shadows, no one watching. Tipping the wounded chair upside down, he wrenched off another leg that had splintered from the impact, and noticed the back had separated, exposing the doweling in the joints. Holding onto the back of what was left of the chair, he kicked at the seat, leaving dusty sneaker prints on the threadbare cushion. After three good boots, the chair came apart with a small squeak.

The pile wasn't big enough. He strolled around the factory floor, scanning for anything made of wood and not nailed down. He managed to find a couple of tubes of rolled-up work plans and one more broken chair. Surveying the pile, he thought better of the pyramid like structure and dragged the chairs out to the sides to build more of a fort, so that air could get underneath and help the fire grow. He jammed paper in between the chairs and tools to keep the flames clawing, remembering the last time the timber had taken a while to catch and all the smoke had alerted the neighbors. The fire department had almost arrived on time for that one. Can't risk that again. He fanned the ends of the twisted newspaper sticks out thoughtfully. Can't risk any evidence. Everything must be ashes. Scorched and brutalized like his conscience.

James took a full hip-flask of 151-proof rum out of his pocket and unscrewed the cap. He held the bottle out and saluted the heap. Grime-splintered moonlight fought its way through the windows and burnished the steel. "To Isabelle," he said quietly, and took a small sip. He breathed in sharply and pressed his tongue to the roof of his mouth as the acerbic liquor burned a path to his empty gut.

He splashed a little of the alcohol onto the edge of the work-bench and watched it dribble down the leg, forming a smeary pool on the dusty concrete. He drizzled a line along the floor to the front door, frugally smearing it with his fingers when the trail sundered and dripped.

At the door, James stood and inspected the set-up, his practiced eye combing the broken debris and mentally stepping through the blaze. The path the fire would take danced in his mind like a silent movie, a vivid collection of festive images, soothing his anxiety and overwriting memories that itched and stung the deepest recesses of his brain. He savored the adrenaline sliding around in his chest.

The lighter was in the front pocket of his cropped jeans. He extracted it, and bent to light the liquor fuse. On the first spark, the alcohol-heavy drink lit up like an orange picket fence and the fire quickly found a victim in the dusty, brittle logbooks. James watched the flames leap from tool to chair to document, like a child under a Christmas tree, finding delight in every shape and rustle.

With some of the furniture properly alight now, the heavy timber table began to smoke. Chips and splinters from years of abuse caught intermittently, making gasping noises akin to

James' own ragged breathing, and blackening the tips of the old table's chisel wounds. As the fire grew and expanded out towards the office at the back of the factory, James slowly migrated from the heat, towards the door.

Comfortable that the blaze was strong enough to stand on its own, he moved through the open door, smearing any fingerprints off the door handle with the sleeve of his jacket. His last glance inside noted the melted light fitting dripping plastic onto the growing blaze, as a bright orange snake inched up the cord to the ceiling.

Creeping back around the side of the building, he scanned the neighborhood for insomniacs before striding tensely back to the hole he'd made in the bush. He could hear the fire crackling and some of the pyramid collapse as he exited the garden in a slow jog towards his car. He paused by a large Elm to look back at his handiwork. The factory was lit up as though someone was crafting a brilliant sunrise inside. Streams of smoke escaped from the louvered windows that were too old and arthritic to close properly. He savored the view with relief and fatigue, his eyes moist with the catharsis. Take it with you, he pleaded silently. Memories of the accident flitted through his mind as he chewed on the inside of his cheek. The taste of blood brought him back from his reverie and he climbed into his car. He didn't put the headlights on until he was over a mile away.

CHAPTER TWO

Elodie had the type of nervous energy that suited over-caffeinated people, but exhausted most others. She was a pretty woman, but wore the pinched look of exasperation most days; her poorly managed need to control her surroundings meant she was low-dosing cortisol around the clock and, thus, slept poorly. She had been in and out of psychologists' offices most of her life. Her particular brand of anxiety meant she was recalcitrant and problematic as a patient, tiresome and unyielding as a friend.

She had a beautiful, slim figure, more egg-timer than hour-glass, which she dressed impeccably in the latest styles and cuts. The 'waif' and 'heroine chic' trends helped her immensely. Her make-up was professional-grade, her cheekbones were desirably high, and her lipstick never bled. Almost every woman who passed her on the street immediately felt worse about themselves.

Elodie sat tensely in the only single chair in the waiting room of Goulding & Associates Psychologists and waited to be called. She never sat on either of the couches, unwilling to take the risk that another patient might sit next to her.

"How are you feeling today, Ms. Doucet?" asked the receptionist brightly.

"Well, thank you," replied Elodie in a polite but perfunctory tone. Not wanting to continue the exchange, she rummaged in her purse for a nail file and began working studiously on non-existent jags.

She had almost run out of nails to unnecessarily re-shape when Dr. Goulding called to her from the doorway of his office.

"You can come in now, Elodie."

He waited while she replaced the nail file, zipped up her bag, unzipped it again to ensure her phone was on silent, re-closed it, stood and smoothed her skirt, and pushed her hair behind her ears. Once sure that everything was in order, Elodie followed Dr. Goulding into his office and sat in her usual spot at the far end of the patients' couch.

"So how are you feeling today?"

"Oh, fine, thank you," Elodie breathed with an insincere smile. "I appreciate you being so flexible this week; I am sorry I had to reschedule."

"That's no problem at all. Life doesn't always conform to a schedule or set of plans, as we've discussed. So, tell me, have you been using any of the tools we worked through last month?"

"Yes, yes, I have, and don't misunderstand me; they are helpful," Elodie extended her hand involuntarily as she spoke, placating, as though she were an employee trying to explain away a late report. "Only, I feel as though we're not getting to the root of the issue."

Dr. Goulding tried to hide his sigh. "Are we missing the root of the issue, or are we ruminating on the issue? Remember our talk about fixation and rumination?"

"Yes, absolutely, and there was great value in that. I just wonder if we're missing something because I still see her so much in my dreams."

"It's quite possible that she'll be a fixture in your subconscious for some time, Elodie," Dr. Goulding ventured, "but that's not going to improve as long as you keep her at the forefront of your waking thoughts as well."

"Yes, but you don't understand. The dreams aren't always a replay of the accident." Elodie looked up from her hands, her eyes wide with curiosity. "Sometimes, she's just there. In the background. I know you say it makes no sense to re-animate the dead. But for all intents and purposes, she isn't dead to me. I mean, I watched her die. I caused her death for god's sake." Elodie paused, the words catching in her throat. "But she's never left me. I don't think she can forgive me. And if she can't, then what hope is there for her family to recover?"

"Her family's recovery is not your concern, Elodie." Dr. Goulding removed his glasses and pinched the skin between his eyes, trying to iron out the dents made by the nose-pads. They had been over this so many times. The Doctor's frustration was reaching peak tolerance with her steadfast refusal to move forward. In the beginning, he viewed her fixation as justified, reactive guilt. But as she skirted around logic and skillfully hurdled pattern-break after pattern-break, he realized the connection and significance she was getting via sympathy had become a lifeline. The guilt had become a 'golden ticket' of sorts. An emotional skeleton key.

He met her eyes. "And why is their recovery not your concern?" She recited dutifully, "Because it's out of my control. Because I can't control other people's perceptions or feelings."

"Correct. But there is a lot you can control. Like your focus areas, how much time you allow each day for rumination, how much time you spend on the tools of your behavioral therapy, and how much priority you give the appointments."

His verbal swipe hit the target and Elodie nodded at the pointed remark, though she continued her train of thought. "I've just never had a sense that this is over. I can't possibly move on when I'm constantly looking over my shoulder."

"But you weren't one hundred per cent in control of yourself at the time, Elodie. You had something of a psychotic break. In the court system, the appropriate course of action isn't prison. It is rehabilitation."

"And I understand that." There was frustration in Elodie's voice now. "But how is that justice? How is it fair that I have yet another fucking episode, someone dies, and the outcome is that they attempt to heal, to fix, to help me? *Help me*, for god's sake! When that woman is dead!"

"The goal is to prevent the crime happening again. You weren't legally responsible for your actions."

"But was I morally?"

Dr. Goulding looked up at the ceiling and sat back in his chair, exhaling loudly. "Elodie, we've played this record. How it was handled is and was out of your control. You were professionally evaluated as not being in charge of your faculties when the incident occurred. We do have to leave that there. What I think we should try is a technique that's become quite popular for reframing traumatic memories. Would you like to try something new today?"

Elodie was absent-mindedly rocking back and forth and chewing on her top lip. She nodded quickly. "Absolutely. Absolutely. I am reliving it constantly, anyway. What's the harm in adding a new spin?" She threw up her hands and laughed a short, shrill laugh. "Let's go. Let's do it."

Dr. Goulding adjusted his posture and settled into his chair. "We're going to go through the incident, but not the way it happened. We're going to do it in black and white, with music, and in the wrong order. We're going to have a go at creating a new physical response and see if that doesn't take some of the edge off your neural response. The technique has garnered some good results with other people and I have high hopes for you. Get comfortable in your visualization pose."

Elodie took off her heels and positioned them tidily to the side of the couch. Swinging her legs around, she lay down with her head up on the arm rest and her legs bent, knees leaning against the back of the sofa. Dr. Goulding waited for her to stop fidgeting. Knowing she released her facial muscles last, his indicator was her brow unfurrowing. Comfortable that she was rested and ready, he began.

"We're going to start at the end. Take yourself back to the scene of the accident. Tell me what you see."

The muscles around Elodie's jaw tightened a little. "I'm standing beside my car at the edge of the road. Her car is upside down in the ditch. It's on fire. I know I need to do something, but I'm frozen. They said when they arrived I was screaming but I can't feel it."

"Good, good." Dr. Goulding shifted in his seat. "I want you to stay with the memory, but make the whole scene black and white. Tell me when it's black and white."

Elodie's eyes flickered back and forth under her lids. "It's in black and white."

"Okay. Now I want you to slowly, as accurately as you can, start playing the scene backwards. I want you to say it out loud as you go so we can make sure it's in the right order. Play the memory in reverse and tell me what you see."

Elodie took a deep breath in through her nose and began describing the accident from the end. "The car is upside down in a ditch. It's on fire. She's on fire. I'm standing on the side of the road and I can hear screaming. I thought it was hers but maybe it's mine. Maybe it's both of us. People are running past me and trying to get to the car but the heat coming off it is too intense."

"Take us backwards, Elodie," said Dr. Goulding, with a little concern on his face. She had a propensity to get lost in the memories and he needed her to focus for this to work.

"The flames are getting smaller. The car is no longer on fire. I'm getting back in my car. I've pulled over on the side of the road. I'm moving backwards in my car, away from the parking spot."

Elodie's voice had quieted with the concentration of running the scene backwards. Dr. Goulding could tell she was watching it like a movie in her mind because her hands were inadvertently gesturing. Her left hand swept across an invisible steering wheel as she described reversing back onto the road.

"I'm back on the road. I'm driving behind her. She's... She's back in control of her car. I'm so angry. She cuts me off. She's gone. I'm driving."

Elodie's hands gently skimmed non-existent controls. She stayed with the vision while she waited for the next step.

"Good, good. Now we're going to run through it in the right order, but with something of a different soundtrack." Dr. Goulding reached for a small CD player on his desk. He switched it on and the sound of polka music filled the room. Elodie flinched at the harshness and speed of the music in what was normally a very calm, quiet, and sober space. Dr. Goulding could see that the volume was grating, but was determined to infuse the vision and break this pattern.

"Take me through the memory, Elodie," he instructed. "Start where you are now, in the car."

"I'm driving," she said loudly, over the ridiculous music. "I'm driving out of town to go for my riding lesson. I'm late and it's making me anxious. Suddenly this car that's supposed to be in the turning lane changes its mind and swerves in front of me and gives me such a fright. I'm so angry. I'm so angry."

"What did you do next, Elodie?"

"I just wanted to give her a fright. I just wanted to let her know she frightened me."

"What did you do, Elodie?"

"I sped up. I got the front of my car alongside the rear of hers and I pulled the wheel hard to knock her. I just wanted to give her a fright."

Elodie was wringing her hands. Dr. Goulding wasn't sure the re-frame was strong enough. He turned the volume up on the stereo a little.

"Keep it in black and white, Elodie. In black and white, remember. Keep the memory moving. Don't justify, just narrate. What happened to her car?"

"I hit her too hard. The car squealed and slid as she over-corrected. She must've thought she was going to end up in the oncoming lane, because she panicked."

Dr. Goulding turned up the volume again.

"Her car went off the road." Elodie forced her story over the strident racket emanating from the little stereo. "The car rolled and rolled and landed upside-down in the ditch. I pulled over as soon as I could, but by the time I was out of the car there were already flames. Someone who knew her must've been following because he pushed past me, screaming her name, but he couldn't get to the car."

"Black and white," Dr. Goulding prompted.

"They're all in black and white," Elodie responded tersely. "The car is black and white. The flames are black and white. The only thing that's different is that I can't hear the goddamn screaming over that fucking music."

Dr. Goulding turned the volume down on the stereo slowly and instructed Elodie out of the visualization. He counted her back to the present moment and she blinked, groggily, as the mundane reality of the office came into view.

He carried the portable stereo over to a cupboard on the other side of the office as Elodie blinked in the bright office lights. Putting it away on a bottom shelf, he smiled. "I think that was beneficial. You're usually much more tense, tearful, and less articulate when you're fully in the memory. How do you feel?"

Elodie sat up. She fidgeted with her cardigan and smoothed her hair down. "I'm tired," she offered without making eye contact. Dr. Goulding looked at his watch. "That's to be expected. Good session today. I would like to see you again next week. I'm interested to know if today's reframe has any impact on your usual flashbacks. If you can keep notes for me please, and make an appointment with Claire for next week, that would be great."

Elodie took out a compact mirror and flicked away a few spots of mascara that had migrated while her eyes were closed. "Next week is fine. See you then."

Out at reception, Elodie confirmed an appointment for the same time the following week and checked her reflection in her compact mirror again. Pushing a few recalcitrant hairs back into place, she smiled tolerantly as Claire struggled to input the next session. "Sorry about this," Claire laughed nervously. "It thinks I'm overriding an existing appointment, but there's nothing there."

"Honestly, it's fine." Elodie's thinly veiled impatience shone through, in spite of her insincere attempt at friendliness. "Why don't you just make a note and then email me the confirmation once you've got it working again?"

Elodie wanted to be home before Damian tonight. She knew her appointments riled him because he saw them as ineffectual, given that her anxiety wasn't noticeably improving. Had he known about the accident he probably would've been more forgiving with time, but Elodie believed the confession could end her marriage. Not just the event, but the concealment of it. Damian thought she was just learning mindfulness and breathing techniques. He had questioned the competence of her therapist on numerous occasions.

Elodie exited through the front entranceway so that she could go back to her car via the promenade and make eyes at the beautiful designer shoes in the windows en route. Something about a well-coordinated outfit made her feel slightly more in control of her day than her emotions could. Her attempts to keep on top of the chaos in her head manifested in obsessive-compulsive tendencies with regard to her appearance and the state of her house. While an immaculately kept home was of some joy to Damian, on bad days she would hover around him with a dishcloth or a dustbuster and he found her need for external order overwhelming.

Elodie reached her car and placed her handbag on the back seat. It was a habit she was creating to lessen her tendency to send text messages while driving. After waiting for another car to pass she climbed into the driver's seat, plugged in her phone and checked a message. A benign comment from Damian about his day; he would be home shortly. She turned up the stereo, blasting nineties pop around the car and joined the traffic flow out of town.

As the streets grew quieter and the traffic eased, so did some of Elodie's tension. She sang along to the radio and tried to leave the therapy session behind her for a bit. Reliving the memory was always draining. She hoped that changing the mental picture to black and white and adding that ludicrous music had rewired something. While the prospect of flashbacks and nightmares did have her constantly on edge, she was genuinely interested to see how they'd look after that experience.

She pulled into the driveway and gathered her things. The garage door was down, meaning Damian had beaten her home. She clucked with disappointment and practiced smiling as she strolled up to the front door. She mentally rehearsed how she would greet him as she entered the foyer. By the time she reached the kitchen she was wearing a contrived glow.

•　　•　　•　　•

"Hello, sweetheart." She kissed him on the lips, with no discernible sense of obligation. Damian responded in kind, obviously pleased to see her emotionally on the straight and narrow this beautiful summer's eve.

Looking down, he admired her outfit of a Chanel-esque suit and silk shirt. "I love this color on you," he said, pushing her pendant out of the way and playfully tracing the deep V with his index finger. He pulled her shirt out a little to see what bra she had on. It was the white one with tiny jewels in the middle of the bows. Excellent.

Damian was particular about details. It was the main reason he had ascended to a management role so quickly; he had remarkable skill at predicting and noticing the tiniest of flaws, a talent he took great care not to exercise at home. He knew Elodie's mother had maintained an impressive level of criticism throughout her childhood so he was careful with his wording, lest he overflow her quota and set off a tantrum.

He gave her another light kiss, and began making a drink. It had become typical of him to start his evenings with a little something on the rocks, as certain projects were moving into the more expensive phases. More money was going out, inevitably more mistakes were being made, and while he wasn't directly responsible for every decision, he was directly responsible for the people who made them. The company he worked for was a design engineering firm that often took on fixed-price, all-inclusive projects, meaning they costed the entire job in exchange for total project control: management through to contractor selection. As Operations Manager, Damian had a hand in every project, and every Project Manager reported to him in some capacity.

How well he managed stress seemed to be more and more affected by the tranquility (or lack thereof) of his home life. He had become extra sensitized to Elodie's moods of late, which left him with a persistent sense of fatigue. This showed itself in a light shadowing under his eyes, and a new habit of skipping his morning shave. His superiors noticed his slightly run-down appearance from time to time, but he wasn't making mistakes at work yet, and like most men, they wanted to avoid having to ask personal questions for as long as they could.

Despite his end-of-the-day slump, he still filled out a shirt well, and Elodie enjoyed watching him move about the kitchen, his dark hair intentionally, artfully disheveled and his tie loose.

"Lunch with the girls today?" he inquired, conversationally.

"Yes," she confirmed, pleased to have been offered a topic other than her therapy appointments. "I was supposed to meet Mother for lunch, but she cancelled and Trudy was able to join me last minute. We went to Stefano's."

Damian plucked a couple of ice trays from the back of the freezer and managed to salvage enough chips from both for his drink. "Fit any shopping in?" He couldn't remember if he'd seen that necklace before.

"No, just a little adoring through the windows today. I didn't need anything but I wanted to stay out and stroll – it was such a beautiful afternoon."

"Good for you, honey." He kissed her on the head and squeezed her waist with his free hand before carrying his drink in to the lounge. "It was a long day. Let me get this down before we start dinner, ok?"

"Absolutely." She smiled serenely, remembering to use her eyes as well. "I'm going to have a glass of red myself."

Damian looked up at her filling the wine glass. She didn't normally have red on good days; red was for calming. "When was your last session with Dr. Goulding?"

Elodie didn't skip a beat. "This afternoon. Why do you ask?"

"No reason." Damian purposefully kept his tone light as well – neither enjoyed this topic. "Was he pleased with your progress?"

"Yes, he was, and we tried a new technique involving music and visualization. He is really interested to see if it makes any difference to my anxiety this week, so I'm to take notes and report back."

"Report back when?"

"Next week."

Damian looked at her for a minute, feeling her silently daring him to comment on the increased frequency of the appointments. Elodie had always gone bi-monthly. She said it was mostly just 'maintenance.' He licked his lips and took the bait.

"That's very soon. Will your appointments be weekly from now on?"

"I don't think so, but it's really up to the Doctor," Elodie replied pointedly. "Besides. It's not about the dates and times, it's about the progress. Right, honey?"

He watched her plonk down heavily on the couch and swing her legs up beside her in an effort to look jovial and non-confrontational.

Damian sighed. "You've been seeing Dr. Goulding for over a year now. I wouldn't think it at all unusual to consider trialing another psychologist if he's not meeting your needs as well as you'd like. Just let me know if you'd like to meet someone else."

Elodie smiled, this time without the eyes. "Ok, honey."

She picked up a magazine off the coffee table and took a long sip of wine, swilling and tasting the whole mouthful so that he could see she was finished talking.

Damian felt as though the point had been made, but he remained somewhat annoyed at her refusal to try another psychologist. In the grand scheme of things, anxiety couldn't be the most horrific thing they dealt with. If they couldn't get nervous people who don't even have jobs through the day, what on earth do they do with sexual abuse survivors? Prisoners of war? He made a mental note to Google the good Doctor's credentials in the morning and see if he couldn't strengthen his case for the inevitable next round of this pseudo-argument. He looked over at her long legs and delicate features, and for the first time since they were married, felt nothing but fatigue.

CHAPTER THREE

The bar was small, full, dimly-lit, and James' boss, Jeff, was already half-cut. The bourbon always gave him a somewhat pressurized glow and the extra weight he carried made everything look an effort. The ends of his hair were stuck to the sheen on his forehead and James tried not to grimace at Jeff's generally excretory appearance.

Jeff and James had been friends for a long time before they started working together. They had met in the last few months of high school, as different cliques split and merged based on where everyone was going after graduation. They shared a similar sense of humor, though Jeff's was more brash and less audience-sensitive than James'.

Recently; however, Jeff's emerging alcoholism had meant he required as much supervision as camaraderie. James wished he'd taken weekly photos of Jeff to track his demise from energetic, hopeful construction worker, to rotund, greasy-haired, reluctant and disengaged business owner.

Jeff had been an incredibly talented builder in his younger years, taking on supervisor duties long before he had officially completed his apprenticeship. But a string of relationship failures and losing his father, who was also a builder and had encouraged him into the role, had proven more than Jeff's demeanor and energy could handle. No longer able to shoulder the sentimental attachment of the role, he had moved away from construction and into cars, which had previously been a hobby.

He had taken over the Brake n' Lube a little before Isabelle died, and he invited James to apprentice there when it became apparent that he wouldn't be returning to university. While his disposition was always broadly upbeat, these days it was likely due more to imbibing than any real sense of fulfillment.

"So, all I'm saying," Jeff summarized, his words gluey, "is that you can't call anywhere a 'Christian nation,' or a 'Muslim nation.' A country can't have a religion. People have religions. I mean, there's a lot of dickheads in this country but you wouldn't say it's a dickhead nation."

James watched him take a swig of his drink with a subtly pained expression. Jeff assumed there was an agreement between them: shared frustration at the bawdy rhetoric he felt he'd so comically slain, but actually James was just silently willing him to stop saying 'Muslim' in the crowded pub.

Jeff's awkward loudness reminded James of his twin sister, Isabelle. She was the extrovert; he was the introvert. She had been the life of every party, with her deliberately hacked-looking haircuts, big smoky eyes and bee-stung lips, perma-drenched in red lipstick. James was the broody, dark-haired wall fly that nursed his drink and hoped social circles would eventually form around him.

In terms of energy, they were two halves of a whole, which made her death all the more painful; James felt somehow that his power source had been taken away. Forever after, he deliberately sought out friends that took up extra space, so that there was someone to do his share for him. Unfortunately, he was not so discerning when it came to *how* they took up said space. In Jeff's case, it was as much through smell as anything.

"You make excellent points," James said convivially, "but I think it's time I got home to the wife."

He downed the last mouthful of beer and checked all pockets for valuables.

Jeff shook out his watch and extended his arm to see the face clearly. Seeming satisfied that James' exit was not a legitimate indicator of an appropriate time to leave the pub, he attempted to flag down the bartender for another bourbon.

Outside in the car park, James fidgeted with his car keys. He'd only had three beers and felt comfortable that he was fine to drive, but he had drunk on an empty stomach and his dexterity was suffering. He reassured himself that the drive home was very short and the long summer days meant it was still broad daylight.

He slid into the driver's seat and started the engine. Paying extra attention to the clutch, he eased the car out of his parking spot and moved toward the exit. The pub filled a large section of a corner block. Patrons entered on one street and exited on the other, meaning James didn't have any traffic waiting to turn in and obstructing his view. A gap in the traffic looked to be a while away. He took the car out of gear and relaxed his left leg.

As he waited, he looked down the street. A series of women's clothing stores gave the impression the shopping district was permanently in some kind of celebration, with their bright colors, contrived party-scene window dressings, and garish sale signs. A blonde with shoulder length hair and a short skirt exited an old building and walked towards James' car. His eyes passed briefly over her legs in absent-minded appreciation, but as his gaze approached her face, something heavy and cold formed just above his sternum and pressed all the breath out of his lungs, pushing him back into the car seat and locking his eyes on the woman in horrified recognition.

Elodie Doucet.

It was Elodie Fucking Doucet.

In his shock, he relaxed both feet and the car stalled with a lurch. He scrambled to press the brake, eyes wide in disbelief. He had assumed she'd be in the institution for years. How long had it been since Isabelle died? It would be ten years exactly in a month. He stared at his shaking hands resting gently on the wheel and tried to steady his breathing. A horn behind him jolted him back to the present and he fumbled with the gears, giving the belligerent person behind him an apologetic wave in the rearview mirror.

He pulled out of the bar's parking lot, drove about fifty meters and pulled over to peer down the promenade. He could just make her out in the distance, turning right onto the main shopping street. He pulled out into the street, rounded the block and entered the congested shopping district a little over the speed limit. Suddenly aware of his shaking hands and beer-breath, he slowed to try and blend back into the flow of traffic.

Outside the pet store up ahead, Elodie was reaching into the back seat of a black BMW. James pulled quickly into an empty parking spot and narrowed his eyes in her direction, sneering at the wealth and comfort she exuded. Retrieving a baseball cap from the foot well of the passenger side, he slid down in his seat, covered his head with the cap and watched as Elodie climbed into her car. She changed the radio station and tidied up her hair in the rearview mirror. James glared. Elodie plugged her phone into the car charger and replied to a text message. James watched the flow of traffic and willed her to pull out in the up-coming break, which she thankfully did. He exited his park, made a slow U-turn and followed her car, keeping a reasonable distance behind.

James' mind was racing. When had they let her out? Had she simply resumed her life as though nothing had happened? She appeared to be doing extremely well for herself; did she work or had she married into money? And the most important question of all: now that Elodie Doucet was demonstrably, disastrously free, what was he going to do about it?

Elodie's car weaved through the congested city streets and headed north. The roads widened and traffic thinned as she led James into the leafy suburbs. His resentment grew proportionate to the size of the houses they were passing. Cussing under his breath, he changed gears roughly, taking his indignation out on the car.

Eventually Elodie slowed and indicated in front of a driveway. James immediately pulled over and slumped down in the driver's seat, watching her come to a stop on a cobbled driveway between manicured gardens with small but ornate fountains. She stepped out of the BMW, collected her handbag from the backseat, and strode towards the front door. James watched her disappear into the house, before squinting to make out the letterbox numbers in the soft amber light of the newly-lit streetlamps.

He recorded her address in his phone and considered getting out of the car. Hers was the only car he could see in the driveway, but the garage alongside it was closed. He couldn't guarantee she was alone. But even if she was, what would he do? What *could* he do? Certainly, she didn't deserve to be living such a wealthy and blessed life. It hadn't occurred to him that she'd ever be let out after such a ludicrously callous act that cost his sister's life.

Memories of that day washed over him. He could smell the smoke. He could hear the screaming. Elodie's or Isabelle's, he could never be sure. He swallowed hard to try and shift the lump in his throat. His red eyes threatened tears. But along with the extreme sadness at the loss of his sister, there was rage. All-consuming, unquenchable rage. His balled fists sat white-knuckled on his thighs as he stared, unblinking at the beautiful glass-front home of the woman who killed his sister. Twice his hand moved towards the door handle. Twice he thought seriously about walking right up to her front door, waiting for her to answer, and then grabbing her by the throat. And twice he pulled his hand back and continued watching the house.

Something had to be done about this.

James put his car back in gear and pulled out into the road.

• • • •

Novella's slip was riding up. She didn't normally bother with layering, but she thought it might stop the floaty fabric of her skirt from sticking to her tights. She hoisted her purse over one shoulder to free up a hand and tried to shake the clingy fabric out. The line at the café inched forward. Novella heard hissing and turned back toward the door. A couple at an undersized table argued under their breath. Novella heard the woman's frustration before she could make out any actual words; they seethed out of her in tense, sharp-edged whispers. "It's not like it's difficult, for Christ's sake. You just have to give a shit."

"I do give a shit!" the man across the table hissed back.

"Apparently not enough," Novella commented quietly, turning back towards the register.

"I know, right?" said a voice ahead of her. "How much does that guy absolutely *hate* his life right now?"

A man in a suit had turned around briefly to smirk convivially at her before stepping up to the counter. "Americano to go, thanks." He counted out change from his pocket and handed over the correct amount.

He was very handsome. Novella attempted to continue the banter. "Actual money! How quaint. I haven't seen that in a while."

"No?" He raised his eyebrows. "You mean because most people pay by card now or are you just unbelievably poor?"

She laughed at his comeback and he ventured a verbal waiver.

"This is where I hastily check your appearance after I may have offended you, and then cringe internally at how awkward it could have been if you'd had a terrible, impoverished upbringing. I'm relieved to see you wearing a blazer and appearing largely together."

"Check in with me again in a month." She smiled. "I'm on my way to a job interview, so if it doesn't go well you can buy my next coffee by way of apology."

A barista with an impressive Mohawk and a giant grin called the man's name. He collected the coffee and lifted it in Novella's direction on his way out. "Good luck with your interview."

She gave a small wave and paid for her coffee, moving to the pick-up area to watch the Mohawk with the lightning hands pump out coffee after coffee at warp speed. A foamy cup of liquid comfort appeared in seconds. She carried it outside to a bench close to where she'd parked that was getting good morning sun. She could see her little car neatly wedged between two Audis. She smiled at her personalized license plate and congratulated herself on a perfect parallel park job. Feeling smug, she slid her sunglasses down onto her nose, pushed her mussed hair off her face, and checked her watch. She had twenty minutes until the interview.

As she nursed the coffee, squeezing her cold hands around the hot cup, Novella thought about James. Even though they'd only been married for a few years she already felt as though her hold on his affections had lessened. She watched a sparrow hopping in a circle on a branch overhanging the sidewalk of the little cobbled backstreet and wondered if she ought to suggest he speak to a counsellor.

Of course, she would go along with him if he wanted, but despite some minor insecurities, Novella wasn't convinced she was the problem. Little had changed between them since their more passionate days; she didn't feel that her appearance or demeanor was any different, and she had only been out of work for a month, not long enough to inflict any financial strain on the relationship.

But he was just so distracted. It seemed as though he was constantly trying to remember something important, and he was so preoccupied with recalling the details that he was missing everything happening in the present. When she tried to snap him back to the current moment, the current conversation topic, the current meal, he seemed annoyed. As though whatever he'd been trying to accomplish alone in his head had been derailed. The persistent preoccupation was no doubt also contributing to their lack of intimacy. Novella tried to remember the last time they'd made love. It must be at least a month. He was always so tired.

She took another sip of her coffee and decided to go into the building early. If she got lost or the elevator was broken she'd need the extra time and she wanted to be in the waiting room well in advance to give the impression of eagerness. Given that this was a Personal Assistant role (Novella's forté), traits such as punctuality, preparedness, energy, and enthusiasm were prized and may be considered along with her actual interview answers.

Inside, the air conditioning was in full force and Novella was pleased she'd brought a jacket. Her slim frame didn't handle the cold well, especially the synthetically icy breeze of an industrial-sized Daikin. Pleased to see that the company's location was well signposted, she took the elevator up to the fourth floor and strode into the stark reception area with a deliberately friendly smile.

"Good morning!" she chirped. The receptionist was a young woman with knife-edge perfect eyeliner and a septum ring. Somewhat progressive for a front of house role, Novella mused as she waited for the woman to finish typing.

"How can I help you?" asked the receptionist with barely feigned interest.

"Hi, Stacey?" Novella read the name badge. "Novella Tallon. I have an interview at nine for the Personal Assistant role."

"Ok, that's with Mr. McRae. His office is the last on the right. If you go through those doors, there'll be chairs at the end of the corridor. He'll come out when he's ready for you." Stacey gestured with minimal enthusiasm, and Novella took the directions with an equally cursory nod and smile.

The office was modern and minimalist. The corridor ran between a row of individual offices with frosted glass fronts. Novella thought that was a clever alternative to the dusty, busy aesthetic of blinds. Money and thought had obviously gone into the set-up and Novella wanted to be part of it. A warmer wall color would've gone a long way though, she thought as she buttoned up her blazer with a small shiver. There's 'clean' and then there's 'sterile.'

At the end of the corridor, as described, there was a row of chairs. She sat in the last one so as not to seem under Mr. McRae's feet the minute he came out to call her. She sipped her coffee, swung her legs with nervous anticipation, and continued pondering James. She was quite lost in thoughts about nice things to do for him when a voice above her laughed. "We meet again!"

Novella jumped up to shake the hand of the man she'd just been talking to in the café. "Oh, that's so funny!" She laughed. "Thank God I didn't push in front of you in the line!"

"Absolutely."

He held the door for her to go into the office and Novella hoped her perfume was noticeable as she passed.

"Imagine how awkward this would be now," he said with a grimace.

"Oh, I wouldn't be sitting here," said Novella, adjusting her unruly skirt for the eighth time and putting the coffee cup on his desk. "I would've left the minute I realized it was you. Lost cause!"

He sat behind his desk. "It's good to see that you have a sense of humor, at least. Now let's go through the credentials."

As he spoke, Novella was simultaneously crafting interview-appropriate answers and making amendments to her memory from the café. The more he smiled, the more she examined his laugh-lines, pondering with some sadness the disparity between how well they suited him and improved his professional appearance, while women were not afforded the same kindness. The way he never looked away from her made her feel flattered and entranced. She hoped her foundation was hiding her blushing, and hadn't sunk into her little crow's feet.

He appeared to have read her résumé in advance, she was pleased to see. She must have been one of the few shortlisted people since he'd actually been given her details by the HR department. He asked good questions and she was happy to explain the scope of previous roles and to take the opportunity to brag a little about some successes she'd had.

Novella had always worked as a PA. Her uncanny ability to remain unruffled in the face of missed deadlines, unrealistic requests, inappropriately demanding bosses, and intensely stressful environments made her the perfect assistant. In addition, it was possible she knew the ins and outs of Microsoft Office better than Microsoft.

Several times he looked visibly impressed at the contribution she'd described and she wondered if he was doing her a charity. She played with her bracelets as she talked. Surely, he wasn't so affected by her minor triumphs in efficiency? Momentarily, she basked in his appreciation before sprinkling in a little office-jargon in an effort to seem experienced and up-to-date. By the time they were at the natural end of the discussion, Novella felt a comfortable camaraderie developing and was not surprised to be offered the job.

"I would love to come and work for you." Her smile was genuine and he responded in kind. She watched him adjust a cufflink that had caught itself on his jacket sleeve as he stood up. "Fantastic. I'll have Stacey email you the paperwork and you can let us know how soon you can start. It's been a pleasure, Novella." He shook her hand, and held the office door open for her.

"Likewise, Mr. McRae. All things going according to plan, I will see you next Monday."

Novella strode down the corridor triumphant and a little giggly. She was ecstatic to have landed a job with someone who seemed so friendly and personable, and wasn't hard on the eyes either.

The thought of his appearance triggered a sudden guilty pang. But that was strange; she hadn't been flirtatious, had she? She didn't think so. Jovial, definitely. Enthusiastic and charming, hopefully. Besides, whatever she was had landed her the job. Overly friendly or not, it was a means to an end. James could tend toward the jealous; she hoped he didn't accuse her of being awarded the job on cleavage alone.

Outside the building, Novella found herself still warm and giddy from the interview as she strolled to her car. She wondered if the butterflies in her stomach were purely from the excitement of landing a new job, and knew instinctively that they weren't. She took a deep breath and tried to push past the excitement tinged with guilt that she felt as she relived the conversation in her mind.

She intentionally brought her thoughts back to James and decided to put on a little show for him that evening. She'd have dinner cooked when he arrived home and greet him with the new lingerie she'd bought a couple months back and not yet found an occasion for. This was definitely a time to celebrate. She couldn't wait to start this job.

CHAPTER FOUR

It was going to rain. Even though it was too dark a night to make out the size or color of the clouds, James couldn't see a single star in the night sky and the air felt waterlogged. He drove home from Elodie's house in silence. No radio, no humming or talking to himself, he couldn't even bear to use the horn when someone changed lanes in front of him without indicating. Every ounce of brain matter not engaged in operating the car was focused on Elodie Doucet, and there was no capacity to field any extraneous data. Part of him was reliving the pain of Isabelle's death on short-cycle repeat, like a scratched compact disc.

But a larger part was actively contemplating how to purge that pain.

James could feel a small tick at the edge of his left eye; he rubbed it roughly with the heel of his hand. He hadn't felt the tick for years and its return amplified his indignation that this whole situation should even exist. Elodie Doucet was a murderer. *Is* a murderer. Elodie Doucet was not paying for her crime. Elodie Doucet had been the splinter in the back of his brain for almost ten years and now here she was, back in town, running errands and going about her fucking day like any other law-abiding citizen. He intermittently drummed out of time on the steering wheel and bounced chaotically between fantasies of strangling her, and forcefully reminding himself that she wasn't worth the jail sentence.

James was completely immersed in his asphyxiation reverie, when a moment too late, his brain recognized the red traffic light and he snapped his head to the left to see an enormous Chevy four-wheel drive bearing down on his driver's side door. He pushed the wheel to the right in panic, but the other driver had already braked, locking up his wheels and skidding to a reluctant stop barely a few feet away, before angrily crunching back into gear and easing around him with exasperation. He bellowed, "Red means stop, asshole!" as he passed. James slowed to a crawl, pulled over on the side of the road, and rested his head on the steering wheel. His heart felt as though it would beat right through his shirt.

Minutes passed. The occasional car sped by and reminded him where he was. For a little while, he forgot about Elodie. But as the adrenaline dissipated, he resumed his status quo, and when Elodie came rushing back in, so did an idea. What if he could instigate her death without actually manually killing her? What if she was driving back to her beautiful home in her leafy suburb in her wealthy part of town and say, for example, her brakes failed?

He took the time to enjoy a vivid hallucination of Elodie living out his recent close-call without the benefit of the Chevy driver's exceptional reaction time. He pictured graphically the exact moment a vehicle twice the size of her black BMW impacted her driver's side door and shoved most of it violently through her smug, deserving torso. He replayed the moment her neck snapped and several major organs split from the force. He envisaged the bruising that would appear over her abdomen as the hemorrhaging slowly diffused to the surface of her skin.

But how would he get to her brakes? He couldn't be seen anywhere near her car. In town was too risky, and he didn't know when she'd next be there anyway. And her home wouldn't work either because neighborhoods like hers had cameras and security lights and elderly people with big noses always peering out from behind floral net curtains, looking for gossip. He was measurably disappointed at the realization that messing with her brakes wasn't realistic.

He toyed with the idea of paying someone else to do it for a little while before coming to the conclusion that he could still be linked to the crime. Sure, he would choose a trustworthy friend, but all dogs bite when cornered and if it came down to a confession or jail-time? He shook his head at the thought.

No way. That was off the table.

So how else could she be involved in an 'accident?' Suddenly he sat back in the car seat, his eyes wide. What if *he* was the accident? What if he was the one to T-bone her? What if it were his brakes that failed? It would involve a bit more planning; he'd need to spend a little time figuring out her schedule so that he could be at the right intersection at the right time. And it would need to be a quiet area so that he could tamper with his car directly after the collision.

He could crack the brake bleeders on each caliper so that the brake pedal went straight to the floor. But then people may wonder why he didn't rip the handbrake up. If he wanted that to fail as well, he'd have to cut the actual brake cables which would start a whole other conversation. Maybe he'd just punch a hole in the master cylinder so that the brake fluid leaked out over the drive. His mechanic's brain began sifting through the technicalities of such an endeavor. He considered the possibility that his occupation and the motive might make him a suspect for a while, but the idea was too delicious to throw away just yet. The energy of it spurred him to start the car and continue his trip home.

As he drove through the quiet suburban streets, peppered with gum trees and fragrant with summer blooms, he stepped through the 'accident.' If he could find a route she traveled often he could lie in wait from a good vantage point and pull out as she approached the intersection. He wondered if it would be safer to just not touch the brake pedal, rather than actually doing the damage beforehand. He didn't like the idea of driving without brakes in case something went wrong. If he didn't brake, there wouldn't be any skid marks, and then he could theoretically jump out and do the damage afterwards to corroborate his story.

His car had airbags and he could better his chances with a prophylactic neck brace. Her car was new so would no doubt have side intrusion bars but they only stopped the car actually busting through the door; she would still take all the impact. The speed limit in residential areas was high enough to break bones if he hit her driver's side. And she was not a robust-looking female. Shouldn't be too hard to snap that neck.

James pulled into his driveway and turned off the car. His excitement would provide good energy for conversation over dinner with Novella. He only hoped he didn't come across too uncharacteristically enthusiastic. He took a few deep breaths and filed the plan in the back of his brain to be revisited tomorrow. He would be back under cars in the morning. He could continue contemplating the smartest option for the brakes then and there. He climbed out of the car and dragged the garbage bins to the side of the house, whistling merrily.

· · · ·

Novella made even slices in four medium sized potatoes and began massaging them in a bowl of olive oil and rosemary. She had been sanguine and energetic since the interview and couldn't wait to tell James that she'd landed the job. She opened the oven and slid the tray of potatoes inside, above the pumpkin she was roasting whole because she couldn't get a knife through it raw. A rush of hot air escaped and she felt her mascara soften. "Shit, shit, shit," she chided the oven, skipping over to the large mirror in the lounge to inspect and carefully separate her lashes. Daintily, she slid a long nail between a pair that had merged their black coating, and tried not to disturb her amateur but earnestly blended eye-shadow.

She had taken great time and care with her outfit and makeup tonight and was anxious to see James' expression when he opened the door. While at the mirror she shortened one bra strap so that they were even and gave her ample cleavage a little encouragement. Her cooking apron hid the suspender belt and panties that matched, but she adjusted them as well, just in case.

Despite her interest in the meal she was preparing and some minor butterflies about the skimpy outfit she'd chosen to greet James in, Novella found herself unable to stop thinking about Mr. McRae. She felt silly for her temporary fixation; she was certain whatever camaraderie she imagined between them this early on, was either illusory or exaggerated. Yes, he was friendly and congenial, but isn't everyone in job interviews? No one wants to seem like they'd be unpleasant to work with or for, she reasoned.

And besides, the conversation was bound to be easy because they already had the exchange in the coffee shop behind them. The ice had been broken. In the space of a single second, she wondered if he was married, cursed herself for wondering about his marital status, and then cursed herself again for not thinking to look at his left hand at the time.

She teetered back to the kitchen on her favorite, most impractical heels. He *was* lovely and tall. And very well dressed. "Novella!" she said out loud to herself as she clipped the ends off the green beans roughly. "Stop already!" She set them on a low heat to simmer and went to pour two drinks at the miniature makeshift bar they had set up at the end of their lounge room.

It was really just a re-purposed entertainment unit, but she enjoyed having somewhere to display her grandmother's crystal brandy decanter that she had inherited, and the tumblers they'd received as a wedding gift. She poured James a double shot of whiskey and herself a coconut rum with pineapple juice. It was her drink of choice on nights out with her girlfriends and it triggered just the right amount of impetuosity. She wanted to be borderline tipsy when he arrived, in case the outfit worked too well; she always felt overly reserved in the bedroom when she was sober, and shoehorned into red satin with lace inserts was no place to be reserved. She took an extra-large sip and almost choked on it as she heard James try the front door handle.

She had locked it because she wasn't wearing enough clothes to risk someone walking in as she was preparing dinner. She hastily pulled the apron strings apart and shimmied out of it, trying not to disturb the clips in her hair.

She made it to the door before he had a chance to get his keys back out of his pocket and whipped it open with gusto. "I've been waiting all evening for you." She purred, her weight on one leg to deliberately accentuate her hips. James stumbled backwards off the porch step, before regaining his wits and realizing his wife was wearing some truly spectacular red satin lingerie. "What? What is this?" he asked, a smile slowly spreading across his face, weary and creased from the drama of the day.

"I thought you could use a little TLC," said Novella, stepping into his embrace as he entered the house with both arms out and a bemused glint in his eye. "So, I've cooked us a delightful roast dinner, *and* I wore a new outfit for the occasion."

"I can see that." He was looking down at her cleavage and trying to see the rest of the outfit without letting her go. She was determined for them to have dinner before he got to enjoy the outfit purely so that she could enjoy him squirming through some flirtatious banter. She stepped gently out of his embrace and turned to walk towards the kitchen. His eyes traveled from the ludicrously high stilettos, up the thigh-high fishnet stockings, paused in glorious shock at the suspender clips, and by the time his eyes were on the lace insert in the knickers, Novella could tell he didn't want dinner anymore.

She plated up their meals. He waited for her to set the saucepan down on a chopping board before physically inspecting the suspender belt. "Where did this come from?" he asked, tracing the stitching down to the clip on the back of her thigh. "A little shop in town," she replied, continuing to busy herself with the dishes. "It's called Weapons of Mass Distraction. They appear to be working." He was trailing kisses down her back.

"Do you want gravy on everything or just the potatoes?" Novella asked over her shoulder, with a knowing smile.

"Don't want gravy." He murmured, trying to undo the clasp on her bra.

"Uh, uh, uh." She turned around to face him. "Dinner first, then you can play. I want to enjoy this facial expression you're pulling for a little while longer. Also, I didn't spend the last two hours in the kitchen to end up microwaving soggy beans later. Go sit at the table."

"Are you kidding me?" He was going over her like she was a newly discovered specimen. Novella rarely spent money on shiny things for herself, she was much more of a home-wares kind of woman, so this was a rare occurrence and it seemed he wanted to savor it. "Novella, I appreciate the effort, but I couldn't give a flying fuck about dinner right now."

"Well that's very flattering." She batted his hand away from where he was trying to pop one of her suspender clips. "But we're going to eat. We're going to eat, and you're going to drink this whiskey I've poured for you, and you're going to keep making those eyes at me, and I'm going to bask in the tension I've deliberately created, and have another rum, and then after dinner we're going to go upstairs and I will tell you what I'm going to do to you when we get there."

James sidled around the table and picked up his whiskey grudgingly. "Tell me now."

She threw him a saccharine smile and sat down to her meal. "No."

"Novella." Her name was a warning.

"Sit down and eat James." She cut up one of her potatoes and spread the chunks around to cool. "Sit down and make charming dinner conversation with your wife, who has news worth celebrating."

He lowered himself into the chair and picked up a fork. He didn't lose eye contact with her bra as he speared a bean and asked, "What news is that?"

"Remember I had a job interview this morning?" She raised her eyebrows. "I got the job!" James' eyebrows raised with a smile.

Novella picked up her rum and pineapple juice and held it out. "To me, and to the holiday we can plan now that we're back to two incomes."

James picked up his whiskey. "Cheers, babe. So, did you buy that outfit to celebrate or is that what you wore to the interview?"

So predictable, Novella thought. "No, honey. I wore a pressed shirt and a blazer to the interview, like all normal people. This set I actually bought a little while ago. I just didn't have anything to celebrate until now."

"Might I suggest that in the future you consider any outfit resembling *that* celebration-worthy in itself?" James took a swig of his whiskey and pushed his food around his plate. "How much of this do I have to eat before we can go upstairs?"

Novella poured more gravy on her beans. "Everything on the plate. Two hours that took me. Two. Hours. Least you can do is enjoy the fruits of my labor." She smiled sweetly. "Now, make charming dinner conversation with your wife while she enjoys her triumphant day and the compliment of her visibly aroused husband."

• • • •

James smiled and continued to eat his dinner. He finished his whiskey and Novella offered him another. He wasn't particularly interested in the drink but she appeared ready to leap up and pour it and he wanted to watch her walk to the bar. She didn't disappoint and he took the opportunity to bask in his own good fortune. He had known from the moment he met her that he was onto a winner. Novella was kind and intelligent with a beautiful figure, and she was empathic enough that he felt completely seen and heard by her in every conversation they had. She took the time to understand him. She wasn't deterred by his quirks; rather, she made it clear that she found his idiosyncrasies entertaining and endearing. He watched her unscrew the cap of the whiskey bottle and remembered the first time they met.

They were at a house party. There was a lull in the group conversation and he had stood up to go get more drinks and she had offered to accompany him to the kitchen and help carry back another round. She was just as heavy-handed a pourer then as she was now. He loved the way she didn't partake in 'awkward silences.' She filled them with humor, with pointless, plot-less stories that were more a collection of one-liners than any discernible tale. She was charming, but for no easily describable reason. He was fascinated by her, purely because of the way she made him feel, as opposed to the content of her communication.

He remembered his drive home, how agitated and malevolent he felt, and compared it to the amorous stupor he was enjoying now. *What are you doing?* he asked himself, shaking his head as he watched her put the whiskey bottle back in its designated spot in the cabinet. *You have such a good life,* he thought, watching Novella sashay back to the table with his drink. She set it down on a coaster and bent down to place a gentle kiss on his neck before returning to her seat.

"Thank you, honey." He smiled at her and took a sip of the drink. She was such a beacon of hope and progress and kindness in his life. Would he really risk it all to get vengeance on Elodie Doucet? The very thought of that bitch was such a dark cloud on the evening's euphoria that he mentally abandoned the whole idea of the fake accident. On the outside he continued smiling at, and flirting with, Novella, enjoying the effort she'd put into her appearance and making double entendres that alluded to things he intended to do to her later. On the inside, he was giving himself a serious lecture about letting the past ruin his future, and the flaw in failing to be grateful for what was directly in front of him.

By the time he'd finished the second quadruple-shot whiskey he was half-cut, sated, and desperate to get under the red satin. He cleared the table and stacked the plates in the sink with one eye permanently on Novella. She finished her drink and started walking towards the stairs. "We can sort those out in the morning." She raised an eyebrow.

He dropped the cutlery into the sink. "Let me at those suspenders." He lunged in her direction and she squealed and bolted up the stairs as fast as the ridiculous stilettos would take her.

CHAPTER FIVE

"Bourbon and coke, and a Heineken, please." Jeff dropped a crumpled bill on the bar and didn't wait for his change. Carrying the drinks over to their pub table, his child-like grin indicated to James that he was already a few glasses deep. His orange polo shirt was decorated with remnants of lunch.

"So how goes it?" Jeff laid the drinks down heavily and immediately took a large swig of his own.

James awkwardly toasted no one, rolled his eyes and then took a small sip of his beer. "Not too bad. I'm not a man to kiss and tell but the wife has certainly been behaving herself of late." He winked at Jeff and fished a coaster out of the carry-all on the middle of their pub table.

"That's what I like to hear." Jeff celebrated with a wave of his glass.

"And now she's got a new job, so that'll take the pressure off. We're thinking of booking a holiday since we're back to two incomes."

"Brilliant." Jeff flicked something off his shoulder. "Where to?"

"Not sure yet. Somewhere warm though. Somewhere I can lie on the beach. Just feel like I need to get away from it all. Been getting a bit lost in the bullshit lately and the change of scene would be a good way to snap me out of it."

"Absolutely. Any bullshit in particular?"

The bar was bustling and a group of new customers split down the middle to get around them. Both pulled their elbows in and paused the conversation as they waited for the wave of patrons to pass.

"Not really." James spoke louder as the hum increased around them. "Just junk in my head. You know how it is. We've all got stuff going on and I'm getting a bit sick of mine, to be honest."

"Amen to that." Jeff clinked James' beer bottle without waiting for him to pick it up. "Nobody likes a broken record."

"Or the smell of burning martyr," added James.

Jeff raised an eyebrow, questioningly. "What?"

"Never mind," said James.

"So, are you going to say any more about it, or do I change the subject?" Jeff shifted his stance.

"I have a beef with someone from a long time ago," James began, "and the intricacies are not important, but basically I'm trying to let it go and concentrate on my life right now, which is, by all standards, pretty damn good."

"But you still kind of want them to die in a fire?" The alcohol in Jeff's system was having a hyperbolic effect on his choice of vocabulary. He nodded, knowingly and sympathetically as though what he just said was a perfectly reasonable option to be considered and supported.

James snapped to attention at the mention of the word 'fire.' "What? No! I... What? Who said anything about a fire? No, I just mean. I don't know if I want to do anything about it is all."

"Like confront them?"

"Yes!" James put his hands out in a gesture of acceptance, relieved to hear a more legal option. "Yes, I am considering confronting them." And ramming my car right through them, he added silently.

"Well, I would," offered Jeff. He'd had enough bourbon by now that 'would' came out sounding like 'word.'

"You 'word'?" James mimicked, hanging desperately on the answer.

"Absolutely. What did they do? Do they need a punch in the throat?"

"Uh. Yeah," said James tentatively. The prospect of receiving an opinion along the lines of what he wanted to hear was too tempting and he threw out a little bait. "They were involved in, that is to say they contributed to," James gestured slowly, trying to soften in advance the reaction he expected, "the death of someone in my family."

Jeff took a step back from the table. "They fucking what? Where are they? Do you need a ride?" He finished his bourbon in a single swallow and picked up his keys.

Horrified, James sputtered, "Did you *drive* here? Jesus Christ Jeff, gimme those." He snatched the keys out of Jeff's slightly sticky, bourbon-scented hand and put them in his jeans pocket. "No, God no, I don't need a ride. We're not doing anything right now. I'm just asking your opinion. Two guys, having a beer, shooting the shit. We're not going anywhere right now." He suggested another round to bring Jeff mentally back to the situation at hand. He realized he would have to buy every drink from now on to ensure Jeff was only drinking singles.

When James got back to the table with more bourbon and beer, he was pleased to see Jeff had poached two recently vacated barstools for their leaner. James passed him the bourbon and hoped he didn't notice it was weaker. "So anyway, it was a long time ago, and I should really have moved past it all, emotionally I mean, not like I don't care that they're dead. But I saw this person the other day and, as it happens, I'm not over it. Not at all." He shrugged and laughed a resigned laugh, electing not to elaborate with any details about following Elodie home.

Jeff was shaking his head and making direct eye-contact. "Hell no. No way."

"No way what?"

"No goddamn way would I be letting that shit go. Why aren't they in jail?" Jeff's eyes were wide and he was pointing directly at James. His sodden brain was impressed at its own Sherlock-like ability to pick something from the story that hadn't been offered. "Why didn't they get a life sentence for jail?" Only one of his eyes narrowed quizzically and James began to regret bringing this up. 'A life sentence for jail' confirmed that Jeff was past his usable limit.

James inhaled deeply. "They couldn't go to jail because they were deemed insane. They got psychiatric care. But it was ten years ago. They're evidently back to their regular life now."

"Lucky them." Jeff mocked, taking a mouthful of his drink. He looked at it suspiciously and James worried he might question the liquor content so he moved the conversation on quickly.

"I know I can't really do anything. But at the same time, I don't know if I can live with them going unpunished. You know?"

"Damn straight. I would've killed them myself." Jeff set his lips in a thin, sneering line and James wondered if he was thinking about someone in his own life who was going to get the same fate he'd intended for Elodie.

'No, you wouldn't,' James said quietly.

"Hell yeah I would. Why would you let that shit go?" His voice didn't rise but the indignation and venom was clear.

"Because you don't want to ruin your life by going to jail yourself?"

Jeff was dismissive. "Fuck that. Only idiots get caught. There's a thousand ways to do it without getting busted. You just have to put the time in at the start."

"You honestly think that?"

"Of course. Look at all the unsolved murders in the news. And that's just the ones we know about. People get murdered all the time and no one goes to jail." Jeff burped loudly. Two women at the table next to them looked over in disgust, but Jeff was oblivious. "The only people who get caught are the ones who don't plan it out properly at the start, and who don't clean up properly afterwards. Cover your bases, and then cover your ass." He patted himself on the rear to help James follow his train of thought, and then burped again.

James was mostly disgusted, but he would be lying if he said Jeff's energy hadn't reignited his interest in the collision plan. He looked around nervously to see if anyone's ears had pricked up at the content of their conversation, but the background buzz had drowned them out nicely.

"I'm not sure it's just about preparation for me, though," said James, thoughtfully. "Because it was a family member I think I'd be first on the questioning list. I mean, because I obviously have a motive."

Jeff mulled this over for a minute. "But you're only one member of the family. Surely everyone in your family wants them dead?"

"Maybe." James was hesitant to divulge too much information, but reasoned Jeff was unlikely to remember too much of this in the morning anyway. "But I was the one who saw her die."

Jeff swallowed hard. "You saw them do it?"

"I was in the car behind them. We were both going to the same place, but we had to take two cars because I always wanted to go home before her." His eyes dropped to the table and he wiped away a condensation ring with his sleeve. "I saw her get run off the road. Her car flipped. There wasn't anywhere to pull over. By the time I managed to get out of the car." His voice broke. "I didn't make it. It was already on fire. She was already on fire."

Jeff was silent. He wanted so badly to say the right thing but he wasn't sure that existed. He put his arm around James' shoulders and gave him a squeeze of solidarity.

"Okay." James took a quick breath in and straightened his posture. Jeff stepped back to his side of the table. "Well, thanks for listening, bud, but I think I'm done. I'm at my driving limit, so I'm going to head home." James swirled the last of the beer in his bottle to capture the foam before swallowing the lot.

Jeff looked serious. "Good luck with it," he said quietly.

•   •   •   •

The evening air was damp from the light showers earlier and James could smell wet earth as he strolled through the bar's parking lot, hesitant to go straight home. He watched a group of patrons exit and cross in front of his car as he sat with the keys in the ignition, but the car still off, deciding what to do in the deep orange glow from the last of the evening sun. Elodie was taking up all available space in his head and he was agitated and resentful that he couldn't enjoy anything these days thanks to her.

He could feel himself going to that place. The place of fixation, rumination, and he knew where it led. He had to get it out, but he hadn't planned a burn for tonight. He climbed back out of the driver's seat and popped the trunk. His tools were always in the car, and the petrol can still had about a liter in it. That would be plenty. He was daydreaming about an old storage shed that Jeff used to drive him to, to inspect imported cars when a voice startled him from his planning.

"You still here?" It was Jeff, artfully stumbling towards him. "That's good. You've still got my keys."

"Oh shit, that's right. Listen I'll give them back to you but you're not going to drive home, are you? I can spot you cab fare if you need it?" James began to retrieve his wallet as well.

"No, no, I'm fine. I'm going to walk. Will stop for a kebab on the way home. It's a nice night now that those clouds have moved on. I do need the keys to get into my house though." He paused, with his hand out.

James toyed with the idea of removing the car key, then decided against it. He'd done his bit; he didn't need to completely mother the guy. "Okay." He closed the trunk, climbed back into the car and started the engine.

Jeff sidled up to the window, dragging his feet through the gravel. James heard a few stones hit the bottom of his driver's side door and cringed. "What were you looking in the trunk for? Don't need a jack, do you? Flat tire?" He leaned back to inspect the wheels. James had a horrible feeling he was prolonging the conversation to bait him into offering a ride, but he had a vulnerability hangover from sharing so much about Isabelle and needed to put some distance between them.

"No, no. All good. Catch you next week!" He released the handbrake and gave Jeff one last perfunctory wave before easing the car forward and praying he didn't run over any toes.

The drive to James' target was short and pleasantly light on traffic. It was a holding shed for pre-certified vehicles on the outskirts of the industrial area of town and rarely had anyone in it. Although he was uneasy about going straight there without any recent reconnaissance, he needed this. Novella wouldn't expect him home from the bar for a while yet.

Approaching the area, he decided to circle the block a few times. He wanted to make sure no work was happening in the shed itself, but he also didn't want to be seen parking by anyone in case they were questioned later. He slid his baseball cap on and sat low in the seat as he moved through the area slowly, his engine at a low growl and headlights on park, scanning for people and activity. Comfortable that no one within smelling distance was working the night shift, he scouted a good parking spot behind a nearby garage and pulled in with his lights switched off.

He cut the engine and sat in the silence for a moment, his mind racing. He was eager to get inside and see what was available as kindling, but he knew better than to rush in. He was aware already that the shed didn't have cameras; that discovery had immediately caused him to file it away as a tempting option for the future. While the shed certainly wasn't his first choice (being quite close to the city), it was turning out to be a half decent backup.

The car made metallic clinking noises as it cooled. Some of Jeff's points about unsolved murders had stuck to James' brain like skin on a hotplate and were replaying themselves over and over. "The only people who get caught are the ones who don't plan it out properly at the start, and who don't clean up properly afterwards." He tapped the steering wheel thoughtfully. If he didn't get rid of Elodie, would she be in his mind forever? Tormenting him every day? If he wasn't past the anger after ten goddamn years then what hope was there?

He needed her gone. She was the trigger, the catalyst, the launch pad for all of his grief, stress, and pain he was reliving.

She killed Isabelle, and now she was slowly killing him from the inside out. Death by a thousand cuts. No therapist would be able to properly extract this anger as long as she was still free and living the high life, while he squandered his time and intellect helping Jeff run his business into the ground. He could talk about the pain until the cows came home, but until that bitch had atoned for what she'd done, there was no hope for him. Elodie got a glass-front home in a tree-lined street, and Isabelle got a box in the cold ground. The memory of his sister stabbed at his chest like an ice pick and he instinctively squeezed his arms around his torso, applying pressure to the wound.

Elodie has to go. Elodie has to be purged. Elodie can't be carried around inside him anymore like a fungating tumor.

Emboldened, James stepped out of the car and retrieved his tools and the petrol can from the trunk. He strode confidently to the door, trying to look authoritative, like he owned the place. He picked the lock on the heavy metal smoke door and entered the abandoned shed, closing the door carefully behind him. Two containers remained at one end from the last shipment, with various car parts inside. There was a BMW logo on the side of the first container and he narrowed his eyes as he was reminded of Elodie's car. His practiced eye sought out consumables and he had compiled an impressive, elongated pyramid of tinder within thirty minutes.

There wasn't time to savor this. Novella might call to see if he was still able to drive home from the bar, and he couldn't stay inside while it caught, lest his clothes absorb too much smoke to air out on the drive home. He splashed the petrol liberally over the kindling, making sure he went right to both ends of the pile and up onto the bottom of the blinds, keeping a little in reserve to make a fuse to the door. Fishing around in his pants pocket for a lighter, he opened the metal door and rested it on his foot. The fire needed fresh oxygen and he needed to be able to step outside quickly to get to his car.

He lit the fuse and watched the orange wave rear up and crash over the pile of furniture and paperwork. The office at the rear had been a goldmine of receipt books, magazines, and outdated, ill-matched chairs. Normally James felt a pang of guilt when destroying paperwork because older buildings could rarely be relied upon to have backed up their information, but the person Jeff had the contract with was a condescending jerk. Fuck him. He should learn how to work a computer.

James stayed long enough to make sure the blinds had caught, and to feel the heat of the blaze on his face. He closed his eyes and took in the scent, transported momentarily back to the scene of the crash and the sensory overload of smoke and screaming and the pungent wafting gasoline that accompanied it.

He breathed in the first few puffs of smoke, light on the air that it hadn't yet saturated, and familiar in his lungs. After a few minutes of practiced enjoyment, he felt a lump in the back of his throat and opened his eyes, taking in the beautiful pile of new embers widening faster than planned. He needed to go. His clothes were getting smoke-logged and the fire was billowing blacker than he had anticipated. There must have been motor oil on some of the items. With the temperature escalating, he yanked the door towards him and stumbled through the opening with his craving met and his eyes streaming. The door hit the bookshelf behind it and swayed gently in the heatwaves while the fire latched onto the external walls and pulled the old building in on itself.

James disappeared into the night.

CHAPTER SIX

The waitress at the cozy, diner-style café was a beautiful Latina woman with a coke-bottle figure and thick, glossy hair. Elodie noticed her as soon as she entered the café, because beautiful women were a favorite target of Elodie's brain. She always compared hair, makeup, and outfit and on this day in particular, she didn't come out on top. The disappointment amplified what was sure to be an extremely stressful meeting: coffee with her mother.

It didn't seem to matter how old Elodie was, spending time with her mother always made her feel like a child. Partly because she tended to divert to submissive in the face of a dominant personality, but mostly because Elodie's mother was a domineering and unforgiving woman who criticized so often it was possibly not even intentional anymore. A derisive tone and intolerant attitude were her modus operandi and seemed as automatic as how she brushed her teeth.

Her mother was already seated in the café when Elodie arrived. Fortunately, her back was to the door so she missed Elodie's full-body sigh of defeat. Even though she wasn't technically late, she was still second, and the raised eyebrows that greeted her indicated it hadn't gone unnoticed. They ordered. Coffee for her mother and tea for Elodie. The drinks arrived promptly; Elodie had chosen this café because there was little to criticize and she hated providing ammunition to someone with such an ample arsenal.

"So how is Damian?" asked Mother, sprinkling the contents of a sugar sachet delicately over the crema. Elodie hated the way she always asked about her via the things and people which apparently defined her. She never said "How are you? How are you feeling this week?" It was always "How is Damian? How is the house? Are you still seeing that Doctor?"

It felt like her mother was verbally refusing to acknowledge that she existed without the context of her things, her activities, her relationships. *Damian is Damian, the house is still standing, of course I am still seeing the Doctor.* Aloud, she said, "Damian is great. Work is going really well and now that the renovations on the house are finished he's much less stressed." She poured out her tea but forgot to use the strainer. Her cup filled with leaves and she sighed and emptied it back into the pot. Assuming Mother was wearing an unimpressed expression, she didn't look up to continue the conversation. "How have you been?

"As well as can be expected, under the circumstances," replied Mother, stirring the black coffee to help the sugar dissolve. She had just had her nails done and was handling everything like it was a dog turd in order not to accidentally smear or dent any remaining wet polish.

"The circumstances?" Elodie asked, well aware that not already knowing was a mortal sin.

Her mother's eyebrows went up in a weary gesture of unnecessary exasperation. "I am referring, of course, to my knee, Elodie. You know very well that I've been having quite significant pain with it."

"Oh right, yes." Elodie was devastated it was a health issue. These were much more weighted, much more unpredictable than anything to do with the house or her social life. She desperately wanted to ask the right question: one with enough concern to convey caring but not condescension, and enough accuracy regarding the timeline to imply that she'd been across this issue since its inception. Conversations of this nature almost gave her an ulcer. She elected to start with, "How is it feeling today?"

"It hurts, of course. I had to walk from my car park so obviously I'm in pain, but I'll cope."

"I'm sorry to hear you're in pain," Elodie said, trying desperately to keep the fatigue out of her voice. "Is there anything I can get you? Has the Doctor recommended anything outside of the pain medications that you need help finding? You know how much I love natural health stores. I'm happy to look at omegas for you."

Before Elodie had even finished the sentence, Mother was already shaking her head. "No, none of that stuff will help. The Doctor has given me some pain relief and now I just suffer until it's bad enough for surgery."

"Okay." Elodie nodded, hoping they were at an impasse.

"So, what's Damian doing to keep himself busy these days?" Mother's eyes lit up as she returned to her favorite subject. She adored Damian. Almost to the point where she thought Elodie was punching above her weight. She couldn't understand how such a good-looking man put up with so much of her daughter's drama, but she deeply respected him for it.

"He's fine." There was hesitance in her voice and Mother picked up on it immediately.

"But?"

"Oh, it's nothing, really. He's fine, we're fine. It's just been on my mind a little that we haven't been as close, recently. But that's normal, right? Couples go through lulls, 'peaks and troughs' et cetera."

Mother took a deep breath in. "I don't know if you can afford to let a man like that get bored, Elodie."

"Bored? No, I don't think he's bored. I just hope he's not feeling like the spark is gone, you know? Because it's not. At least for me."

Elodie was nervously playing with the sugar sachets. She over-wrung one and it burst, sending sugar crystals all over her side of the table. She immediately began scooping them up, but once her hands were full realized there was nowhere to put them. She tried to make a small pile on the side of the table.

Her mother watched her awkwardness with a disapproving stare. "What I mean is, I don't think it's a good idea to let your level of effort slip. A man like Damian has options, Elodie."

Elodie was hurt, but not surprised. "Intimacy requires effort on both sides, Mother."

"Well of course, but Damian has a job. You are the one with time on your hands. Don't you think it would be nice if you used some of that time to pick up some decent lingerie and make yourself available?" Mother took a sip of her coffee and waited patiently for Elodie to give her the answer she wanted.

"It's not just about time, though is it? It's about energy, and chemistry, and desire. The issue isn't that I don't have time to dim the lights and meet him at the front door with no clothes on." Mother winced at the unnecessary vulgarity but Elodie continued her train of thought. "It's that the urge hasn't struck. Both of us, I mean. We used to be at each other all the time. These days it's like there's no electricity between us."

Mother pushed her empty cup away and the waitress swooped on it immediately. "Electricity doesn't generate itself. It requires effort and commitment. And since you're the one who has all day to deal with that, I don't see why it's so unreasonable to expect that you could go a little more than half way. I mean, surely your marriage is important to you?"

"Important to me?" Elodie was temporarily floored by the understatement. "Of course, Damian's and my relationship is important to me. It's the *most* important thing to me." Elodie wanted to add "Don't be a tiresome idiot," but elected to leave it there and pour some more tea. Thankfully this time she remembered the strainer.

"Well then." Mother gestured widely as though the problem had been solved. "It won't be too much trouble to go the extra mile and get this aspect of your relationship back on track. Will it." The last part wasn't a question.

Elodie nodded, feeling rebuked. "I'll give it a try. Thanks, Mother."

•   •   •   •

Damian was late. Several deadlines had been missed on a contract with a major client and he'd been in damage control mode all afternoon. He was weary and in need of a drink when he pulled into his driveway, so much so that he couldn't even find the energy to put the car in the garage. He came inside briskly, shedding jacket, tie and briefcase in a whirlwind of disburdening that caused Elodie to leap up from her chair and begin collecting things as he went.

"You're home late," she began. "Was it a bad day?"

"I've had better." Damian was already getting ice out of the freezer for his drink. "Lots of stupid people making stupid mistakes and not letting me know about them until it was too late to do anything. I think I sorted most of it out but we'll be in the dog house with the client for a bit." He poured a gin and tonic and took a big mouthful before indicating in Elodie's direction with it. "You want one?"

"No, I'm good thanks. I have tea."

He moseyed into the lounge and collapsed on the sofa, limbs in four different directions. His drink sloshed on the upholstery and he made no effort to sponge it up. Elodie clucked, pained at the chaos. He rolled his eyes. "Don't start Els, it's clear and it's booze. It doesn't mark and it'll evaporate." He took another swig and laid his head back on the arm of the sofa with his eyes closed. The ice in the glass clinked musically.

Elodie had been ruminating on the conversation with her mother all afternoon. The sense of obligation she'd drawn from their discussion was immense and as she sat in the armchair looking anxiously at her exhausted husband sprawled across the couch, she was overcome with guilt. She stood up and approached him. Because of his awkward posture she wasn't able to see a way in, so she sat down on the floor next to the couch and clasped his hand.

He opened his eyes and looked down at her. "What's up?"

"Nothing." She smiled. "Just pleased you're home."

"God, me too." He sighed, reclining his head back onto the sofa arm. "What a fucking day."

Elodie was uncomfortable sitting on the floor but there wasn't room for her on the sofa. She was pleased his eyes were closed because she'd never felt so graceless and inept. It wasn't usually an issue getting Damian interested in sex, but she didn't feel she could wait for a more natural moment. What if he passed out on the couch? She would miss her opportunity, which somehow had so much more urgency than usual. Her mother's words were at the forefront of her mind.

"I don't know if you can afford to let a man like that get bored, Elodie."

She ran her hand up his arm, sliding her fingers up under his rolled-up shirtsleeves. She felt bumbling. He didn't move. "Do you want to go to bed?" she asked, hopefully. His eyes stayed closed. "Not yet. I'm tired, but I'm not sleepy. Just let me finish my drink, okay?"

She let go of his arm and sat cross-legged on the floor for a moment, drawing patterns in the plush carpet and deciding whether or not his response constituted rejection. She can't have been rejected, she reasoned with herself, if he hadn't opened his eyes yet. *Just let him finish his drink for god's sake,* a harsher voice instructed. She waited. Eventually he sat up for better access to his G&T. Sensing her opportunity, she scooted up onto the sofa and leaned against him. She was momentarily delighted when he put his arm around her and kissed the side of her head, before taking another mouthful of his drink.

"How was your day?" he asked, realizing she might be acting a little clingy for a reason. "Coffee with your mother this morning, right? How did that go?"

"The usual," Elodie answered. She didn't want to start talking about her mother right now. Nothing would get her out of the mood for physical contact faster than a stress reaction. "I've been looking forward to you getting home." She attempted to say it in a seductive way but it came out a little vague.

Nevertheless, he took the bait. "Have you now?"

She lifted her face up towards his. He realized what she wanted but she only received a cursory peck before he returned to his gin. Undeterred, she rested her hand on his thigh. She felt awkward and uncoordinated; this was so much easier in the bedroom where they both got undressed and drawing attention to one's physicality was simple. Trying to make herself available whilst fully clothed and seated in an awkward position wasn't working at all. She considered going upstairs to change into lingerie but just as she was about to get up he said, "I'm going to make another G&T and maybe put a movie on. I'm fucked, but I'm too wired to sleep. You can head up whenever you like, though. Don't wait on me."

Elodie felt like crying. Normally Damian being disinterested in love-making was a relief because she rarely had the energy herself, but a whole day of fixating on the concept of losing him over it had worn her down. All day she had told herself she was going to be the good wife Damian deserved. He worked hard; he provided for her beautifully. The least she could do was demonstrate her love and gratitude. She rubbed at the damp spot on the arm of the couch where his gin had spilled earlier.

A little piece of her was devastated that she'd let her mother's comments drive her actions, culminating in a spectacularly unfulfilling exchange. Some of her was offended that Damian had been implicitly offered her body and seemed indifferent, and the rest of her was just so, so tired. The part of her that was overtired made the unfortunate decision to voice its disappointment with a throwaway shot. "Well, if you decide at any point that you would like to spend some time with your wife this evening, then you know where I'll be."

Damian rolled his eyes, clearly annoyed at her remark.

She turned off the lights in the kitchen while Damian was getting more ice out of the freezer and made her way up to the bedroom. She heard him sigh at the juvenile action.

'Hurt Elodie' felt justified in the parting comment; he had been at work all day and he should want to cuddle up to his wife when he got home, no matter how tired he was. 'Logical Elodie' felt instinctively that the comment was unnecessary and made the situation much worse. 'Logical Elodie' turned out to be right on the money.

•   •   •   •

Damian closed the freezer, put the ice cube tray on the counter and walked over to the wall to switch the kitchen lights back on. The idea of going up to bed anytime soon was deleted from his priority list. He finished making another G&T, then he put on a movie, and eventually he fell asleep on the couch.

CHAPTER SEVEN

Jeff was sitting in the office eating a sandwich and reading the paper when James came in, wiping oil off his hands and looking sheepish. His left work boot stuck to the floor as he entered and he looked down to see a dried puddle of coffee extending out from the sink. "Hey, you got a minute?"

"Yeah?" Jeff said through a mouthful of egg salad on rye.

James moved out of the puddle. "I just finished up the truck, so I'll move it out to the pickup area, but are we good if I don't start that engine mount until tomorrow? I forgot I have a dentist appointment this afternoon and I need to get out of here shortly." He looked at his watch and tried to sound matter of fact with a hint of contrition.

"Yeah, you're good." Jeff kept his eyes on the paper he was reading. "The engine mount is for a project vehicle. He won't stress if it's in for a couple more days. You getting anything serious done?"

"Uh. No." James tried to quickly think of something dentists do. "Just a clean and a checkup. Some sensitivity in the back, just want to make sure there's no holes and stuff. Y'know."

'All good. Have fun. Hope they're not too hard on the wallet."

"You and me both," James said with a forced laugh. He closed the door to the office and went to wash up.

The traffic was terrible and James was short-tempered and liberal with the horn. He wanted to get back outside the building he'd seen Elodie exit last week. He'd driven past it on the way home from work a few days ago and noticed that it was a shrink's office. Surely someone with her issues would be on a regular schedule? He had given himself enough time to sit and wait for a couple hours either side of when he'd last seen her, just in case.

Jeff thought he was at the dentist, and Novella thought he was at the pub with Jeff tonight. Donning his old black cap, he put the sun visor down and slumped in the seat. He had a good parking spot far enough up the road to be inconspicuous, but close enough to see who was going in or coming out. He wished he'd thought to bring a takeaway coffee with him while he waited. He was too anxious to eat but he wanted something to nurse to pass the time. He settled for turning the radio up, as he waited for Elodie to appear. He was visibly excited about this stage of the reconnaissance. Planning was a type of organization and he felt its therapeutic benefits almost immediately.

The minutes ticked by. James' eyes darted up and down the street, afraid he'd miss her in the crowds. Occasionally someone would pass the car and give him a dirty look for taking up the parking space when he obviously wasn't going anywhere. "Fuck off," he muttered quietly under his breath whenever he spotted them. Every time a blonde with shoulder length hair appeared he sat up in the seat, his heart rate quickening. At least twenty times it wasn't her, and he had to revert to patiently watching.

Suddenly, a bright pink jacket caught his eye. He knew instinctively it was her, even before she turned her head for him to confirm. He pushed the sun visor up and followed the flash of pink as it stepped across the path of several other pedestrians and made its way up the stairs into the office. He couldn't believe his luck. It was a regular appointment. He felt triumphant, and suddenly extremely impatient. This was excellent. He rested his elbows on the steering wheel and tapped his head with his knuckles in excitement. He needed to move. Now that she was in the office he felt confident that he had at least thirty minutes, probably an hour to kill. He decided to pop into the convenience store for that coffee and to use the bathroom. He almost skipped up to the counter, and dropped several coins on the floor as he tried to pay.

Back in his car, he sipped the coffee slowly and wished he'd bought tea. The caffeine was harsh on his stomach, which was already agitated by all the butterflies. People continued to pass by the car, and James continued to drum energetically on every surface. Several times he had to put the drink in the cup holder so that he could use both his hands to bleed off some of the nervous energy. His head nodded a consistent beat, even when the radio station was in between songs.

The hour felt like years, but eventually Elodie exited the office and James was ready. He had anticipated the time and his cup was in the holder, the visor was back up, the radio had been off for about 20 minutes to preserve his battery and the keys were in the ignition. She crossed the street, got into her black BMW, and started the engine. James started his engine as well and put the car in gear. His heart was racing and his mouth was dry. He momentarily regretted not buying water with the coffee but before he had time to get properly annoyed, Elodie had pulled out of her parking space.

James followed, paying close attention to her route, even though it was now familiar. He didn't want to forget a single detail.

He was pleased to see she didn't like the freeway. The more time she spent in residential areas the more options he had with regard to intersections. Every time they stopped at a red light he was scanning for roads with plenty of parking space. Whenever they moved through a quieter area he recorded the street names with his phone so that he could come back to the areas later and choose the best bet.

The further they went, the more excited he got. There were so many options. His focus wavered a little as he visualized the moment right before impact. The feeling of exhilaration he expected to feel as his car sped towards her door. The look of abject terror on her face in the last few seconds before she was pulverized from the inside out.

He wondered whether he should have his lights on even in the daytime, to ensure he could see her expression clearly right before contact. He wanted her to be utterly terrified. He hoped her heart jumped into her throat and her insides liquefied from fear. He hoped she was able to recognize his face in the split second she had to process him before her neck snapped sideways. He didn't particularly want her death to be quick and painless, but he wasn't willing to give up the violence of his chosen method. He departed his reverie to record another address.

They were within a couple streets of her home now. James slowed down, pulled over, and let her carry on alone. He checked the recording of the addresses on his phone and made a mental note to plot the most appropriate options on a map when he got home. He could scout them for parking spots on the weekend. For now, though, he had the information he needed.

As he drove back to the pub, he started a shopping list in his head. He liked lists. He liked the certainty of knowing he couldn't forget something as long as he had ticked everything off. He liked the assurance they gave him about his preparation. Checking off the last item almost felt like praise in itself. He would need a neck brace to better his chances on impact. He assumed the airbag would do most of the work but it wouldn't hurt to be extra prepared, he mused, smirking at the pun.

He also had to finalize what he was going to do about the brakes. He was fairly confident that he could replicate wear and tear, but he felt it prudent to take into account the confusion, adrenaline, and potential shock he might be feeling directly after the collision. He would also need to put serious thought into the right tools for the job, since it would be naïve to rely on dexterity at that point.

By the time he got home it was dark, and he was weary but wired from the hours of nervous energy. He contemplated telling

Novella he'd been to the dentist as well, just in case that story ever needed to line up, but decided against it. Jeff and Novella never had reason to speak. And the less he had to engage tonight, the better.

•   •   •   •

Novella was excited to discover her new colleagues had Friday night drinks and she had dressed accordingly that morning, using several layers to make sure she was still meeting the office dress code during the day, but could show a little skin when they got to the bar. She was hoping for some kind of social event to help break the ice with everyone she hadn't met yet, and also give her a chance to talk to Mr. McRae in a relaxed, less professional setting.

She and Mr. McRae had plenty of dialogue in the office, but it was restrained by the work and professional environment. Novella was embarrassed to discover she had formed something of a crush on him, and while she obviously didn't intend to do anything about it, it made the workday interesting. She was not secure enough to believe that he might also notice the tension, and so she was comfortable enjoying the balancing act of choosing her words and actions in the office so as to come across one smile short of flirtatious.

She was pleased to discover that the work was well within her capabilities, too. In the past, she'd taken assistant roles for several managers at one time, so only being responsible for one diary and one set of papers could be done without any stress on her part. She was in her element, organizing and directing, and she took particular joy in using a directorial tone with him.

"I'm going to need six signatures from you before you go to lunch."

"It's a client lunch and we're scheduled for one o'clock precisely – the signatures will have to wait."

"I already rescheduled everyone for one-thirty because I knew that meeting would run over. Take a seat."

She continued to refer to him as Mr. McRae, long after the relationship had become familiar enough that she could've used his first name. Partly because it tempered the content of her instructions when she needed to be firm; one could never say she wasn't being respectful. And partly because he seemed to like it. Novella knew men had much more sensitive egos than they'd ever admit, and a little implied authority went a long way.

The bar wasn't far from the office, so Novella left her car in the staff parking lot. She only intended to have two drinks with some food so she could still drive home. Before she left the office, she removed a long-sleeved top to reveal a spaghetti-strap dress, and touched up her makeup. She was excited for the beautiful rosy feeling the first half glass of wine produced, and about chatting to the people she'd seen around the office, but hadn't been able to introduce herself to yet, with alcohol lubricating the flow of conversation. In the office, you needed a reason to open a dialogue with someone you didn't report to or work with directly. In a bar, one's very presence was considered sufficient reason to say hello. She added another coat of mascara and pushed her hair into place.

The bar turned out to be a quaint country-style tavern with long picnic tables and a timber-heavy aesthetic. Mounted on the walls and along the ceiling beams were old, rusted farm implements. The bar itself was long and deep; little effort had been made to clear the knots and splits in the original tree-trunk and Novella found the simplicity of the look charming.

There was a comprehensive selection of bar snacks, which Novella appreciated. She ordered breads and fries immediately, to help soak up the alcohol as she set about getting a glow on.

As if inveigled by her enthusiasm for starchy carbs, Mr. McRae came and stood next to her at the bar as she was ordering. After she had rattled off her list, he passed a company credit card over the bar and instructed the bartender to start a tab. "And I'll have a Kronenberg, thanks."

Novella was jubilant. "The company covers our Friday night drinks?" she squeaked, incredulously.

"Not usually." He grinned. "But I'm well under on my usual spend and we've put in a lot of extra work this week making it up to GypCo., so we should celebrate. A few rounds and some fries won't kill them."

"I also ordered breads." Novella deadpanned.

"You're fired," he replied.

He smiled down at her as she laughed. She hadn't worn heels today and she was a lot smaller than she usually appeared. Their drinks materialized and they carried them over to the largest table in the middle of the bar where the rest of the group were half sitting, half milling about. All the cliques had separated and everyone was laughing and starting the psychological extraction from the work week. Ties were loosened, swipe card lanyards were being shoved into purses, and extra lipstick had been applied.

Novella could pick up various portions of weekend plans being explained. Someone she didn't know mentioned skydiving which immediately drew her attention and she stepped around the table into their group. "Will this be your first time?" she asked with a big smile and genuine interest. A tall woman in a charcoal pants suit returned her friendly expression and welcomed her into the conversation. "It is, yeah." She nodded nervously. "I can't wait, though; it's been on my bucket list forever. Plus, all my friends have done it and they all raved, so I know it's going to be the biggest rush."

"Yeah, that's what I heard, too." Novella nodded enthusiastically. "You'll have to let us know on Monday how it went."

"Assuming you survive," added someone else, which was immediately greeted with several playful slaps and a disdainful, "Alice! Jesus Christ. Trust you."

Novella laughed and tried to make amiable eye contact with everyone in the group, in the hope that those who found her unfamiliar would offer a hand and a name. The drinks in everyone's hands eased the ebb and flow of people moving in and out of conversation topics and helped the discussion move along. Soon she was telling stories and jokes as though she'd known them all for years. Only when she finished one particular story about a backpacking trip from her early twenties did she realize Mr. McRae had joined the group and was standing beside her. She was relieved when someone picked up where she finished and used her story as a launch pad for a similar one because she was suddenly unsure of what else to say.

It was quite nerve-wracking, she realized, to have him as an audience in a social setting like this. She didn't have her blazer and her glasses for armor here. She didn't have her conversation topics provided for her via work orders and schedules. All of a sudden being near him in a bar was less exciting, more unsettling. She finished the wine in her glass in a large gulp and tried to focus intently on the new speaker, all the while wondering what to do about the warmth in her left arm from him standing so close. He noticed her empty glass and asked if she wanted another. *Hell yeah,* she said in her head. "Yes, please," she said out loud.

He walked to the bar and put two more drinks on the tab. He was back quickly so Novella's pulse never got a chance to settle down. He placed the glass in her hands slowly and deliberately, taking his time letting go. She felt the warm skin of his hands as she closed her fingers around the bowl and focused all the dexterity she could muster on not dropping it, despite the slippery condensation coating. "Thank you." Her voice sounded strange in her own ears.

Alice was telling her own story about a wedding she'd gone to recently. Novella found herself following the detail of the story quite intently, in order to ask a pertinent question at an appropriate time. She was sure that friendly conversation wasn't supposed to require this much physical effort, but a large portion of her brain was jumping up and down in Mr. McRae's direction, being overly excited that he was standing there.

The wine was making it difficult to fake nonchalance. She gave the giggly, nervous part of herself a stern talking to. *He is your boss. He is married. YOU are married. Nothing will be happening. Fantasies are one thing, but not all this tension crap. Now turn around, and talk to him like you're both normal human beings who work together for fuck's sake!*

The reset button effectively pushed, Novella turned and looked up at Mr. McRae with an intentionally relaxed expression. "So, do you think we're in the clear with GypCo. now?"

He waved his hand in a fifty-fifty expression. "I think so. They were furious about the delay, but they must be used to contractors by now, and we have gone above and beyond in terms of effort to remedy the situation, so" He nodded. "I think we'll be fine. We've definitely used up our credit, though."

"Hmm." Novella nodded thoughtfully, trying to give the impression she cared at all about GypCo. "Yes, we'll have to get those communications issues sorted quickly. Presume the people at fault have been advised of next steps?" The bland topic was working well. Their interaction was flowing nicely and she was able to enjoy the banter without the stress of having to think of something witty.

Mr. McRae swirled his beer absent-mindedly. "Oh, yeah. They know they screwed up. For one or two of them it was a second warning, so I'm comfortable that we shouldn't see too much of this cropping up for a while. So, what about you? How are you enjoying the new job?"

"It's good, but I suppose I have to say that because I'm talking to you"

"So, you're lying to keep me happy?"

Novella swore there was a hint of flirtation in his tone, but she didn't allow herself the credit of his perceived affection.

He's married. He doesn't like you; he likes his wife.

Her internal dialogue prodded her temporarily piqued ego. "Not at all. The job is great. Actually, it's a lot easier than my last one so I am genuinely enjoying it. You're not difficult to manage at all." She took a sip of her wine and let the words hang.

"I'm pleased to hear that." He paused without breaking eye contact and the butterflies came back. Her hand went instinctively to her stomach in a placating motion. *Please god don't let me puke on him,* the inner dialogue pleaded.

"Because you're probably the most efficient PA I've ever had," he continued, "and I really enjoy working with you."

Compliments made Novella uncomfortable enough, without having them come from someone she had been picturing shirtless in a crowded bar after one and a half wines. She needed to rein this in. The tension had already exceeded the limits of 'appropriate,' as far as she understood it. Her little infatuation hadn't registered as an issue before because she was one hundred per cent sure it was one way, but the tension in the room was unmistakable now. Her arms were warm and her heart rate was up and suddenly she was thinking of James and feeling like an idiot. "Thank you," she said quietly, breaking the eye contact.

She turned and moved carefully back into a clique next to them, where a guy from the accounting department was explaining in great detail what sports bike he'd just purchased and why. Novella pretended to be intensely interested in custom graphics for fairings and hoped Mr. McRae would do the same, but he elected to follow her and once again she found simply listening to a social conversation incredibly labor-intensive.

She missed at least every second sentence because her mind was so aware of him, casually sipping his beer and occasionally making a well-timed, relevant comment. Novella couldn't help feeling as though he knew what he was doing. He seemed very relaxed on the outside, but the electricity he was projecting had to be intentional. Either that or her minor 'crush' on him was a lot more serious than she'd imagined. She finished the second glass of wine and excused herself to the ladies' room.

Inside a stall, she sat down on the commode and clasped her hands together. She took a couple of deep breaths and thought about how to handle the rest of the evening. Her head was swimming and she realized with a jolt that she'd forgotten to eat any of the fries and bread that she'd ordered. The wine had hit her empty stomach and, finding no doughy appetizers to soak it up, continued merrily into her bloodstream at warp factor three. She couldn't drive home like this. She'd need to eat a heap of food and sink a couple waters before leaving. It wasn't late; she would still be home before ten. Pleased to have a simple plan to leave with her dignity intact, she finished up in the bathroom and was just about to stroll out to the bar when she realized she hadn't checked her phone all evening.

An uncomfortable feeling that perhaps her husband had been trying to reach her while she was flirting with her boss washed over her as she rummaged around in her handbag. Pulling the phone out, she stabbed at the home button and waited for it to light up. It was almost four years old and did everything like an arthritic grandparent. After a torturous few seconds the home-screen illuminated with the time, date, and nothing else. No messages, no missed calls.

Novella let out a sigh of relief coupled with a tinge of annoyance. She'd reminded James about their impending anniversary the day before in the hopes that he'd take the hint and make some kind of effort but he'd seemed disinterested. Her blank phone compounded the irritation. She dropped it back into her bag as she pushed the swing door to exit the bathroom. Mr. McRae appeared seemingly out of nowhere holding a glass of wine in her direction. "I got us another round," he said, cheerfully.

"Oh, I can't. I'm sorry. I was just about to order a water. I'm driving," she said with an apologetic tone, wincing in the direction of the offered glass. The part of her brain that had been jumping up and down in his direction before desperately wanted to take the third wine and see where it led, but she continued to ignore the urge.

"A water? On a Friday night, when the company is paying? Where's your sense of adventure?" He held the wine out to her again. "Come on. You don't need to drive. I can give you a ride home when we're done."

Novella's mind immediately pictured a thousand things she didn't want to see or think about. She shook her head briskly in an effort to bring her attention back to the external, in the present moment. "Oh no, I couldn't impose. I'll just drive."

"Nonsense. I can have four and still be under the limit; by my count we're only up to three. The office parking lot is safe enough overnight. Besides, you can't have met all the staff yet?" He led her over to a different clique and briefly introduced her before asking someone called Zach to tell everyone about his recent trip to the Galapagos Islands. As Zach leapt at the chance to recount the highlights of his holiday, Mr. McRae took one of Novella's hands, lifted it up and wrapped her fingers around the wine glass he'd been carrying for her.

She desperately hoped no one saw the perilously improper length of time he took folding her fingers around the bowl of the glass. In reality it was a second, but to Novella it seemed like minutes and she could still feel his hand on hers. She glanced briefly up at him to see if he was showing any signs of being affected by the tension. He didn't look back down at her, but she could see a small smile curled in the corners of his mouth.

You rat bastard, thought Novella, realizing he was absolutely aware of the air between them, and that he was enjoying it. His one small gesture completely modified her internal narrative that all parties were equally nervous. *He was doing this on purpose. It was a game!*

At the start, she had developed a crush she felt slightly guilty for, but believed it to be totally one-sided and therefore no harm, no foul. All adults fantasized. That was a part of life, and it certainly made her look forward to work, which was no small feat. Take the wins where you can get them, she had reasoned. But that was then. It was different now.

This is only going to be a problem if you're not careful about who sees, she thought to herself in a haze of wine and boosted confidence. *If he wants to stir the pot, then let him. I can flirt with the best of them. As long as I don't actually touch him then where's the harm?* Her ego was in full control now. The realization that he was voluntarily playing this game was unbelievably flattering.

He was an exceptionally good-looking man, and although she was a (mostly) happily married woman, she didn't want to turn down what she expected would amount to a few sly looks, a couple of throwaway compliments, and a sense of attractiveness that, if she was honest, she didn't feel enough in her daily life.

Her butterflies had been replaced with the excitement of a new connection. She wanted to play her turn. Looking up at him again, she leaned in and whispered innocently, "I haven't been to the Galapagos. What does he mean by 'archipelago'?"

Imperceptible to anyone else, she got the result she was after. In the moment of eye contact, his pupils dilated noticeably, and he blinked a couple of times before answering. "It means a group of islands." Such benign content, such intense eye contact throughout. She nodded. "Oh, I see. Thank you." She broke the eye contact first, had a sip of her wine, and moved her weight to the other foot, so that her sleeve gently brushed his. Zach continued raving about turtles and everyone else was enthralled.

Novella ate some of the fries on the table behind them, but she was too busy thinking up legitimate questions and conversation topics to eat as much as she needed to, to soak up the three (or was it four?) glasses of wine she'd consumed. In the back of her mind, a little voice kept piping up and reminding her that she'd been talking to Mr. McRae for upwards of three hours and she better hope no one was paying attention. She needed to go and find someone else, preferably a female, to talk to, but she couldn't tear herself away from the intoxicating connection, and he seemed to be making no effort to either.

One by one, the others departed. All too soon, it was past eleven pm and they were saying goodbye to the last colleague. "I hope you're still able to drop me home." Novella said, her cheeks flushed from the wine and the attention.

"Yes, of course. Let's go." They set their empty glasses on a table and he touched her on the shoulder lightly to direct her towards the door. She didn't think she was stumbling, but she felt very light on her feet, almost buoyant. She focused all her attention on walking a straight line to the exit, simultaneously very aware that he was walking behind her.

Once outside, he spoke. "My car's still over at the office. Are you okay to walk back or should I drive over and collect you?" He smiled teasingly at her obviously tipsy state.

"I can walk!" She was playfully indignant. "I'm not ruined, just glowing." She said the last word fancifully, with expansive hand gestures. It was true; she felt wonderful. She'd drunk enough wine that everything was excellent, but she was still probably another whole glass away from swaying and inappropriate. She congratulated herself silently on hitting the pinnacle of inebriation and noted with extra pride that she still had all her belongings and hadn't said anything incriminating. And now she had a ride home with someone whose company she was thoroughly enjoying.

In addition to the alcohol, the situation itself was quite intoxicating. She was deeply flattered by Mr. McRae's attention; she felt special. She felt uplifted. She felt seen. There were small, dull pangs of guilt about James in the background, but she drowned them out with her belief that this wasn't going to go any further than banter. Than eye-contact. Than tension. James would never find out about these conversations, these flirtations, and they made Novella happy. She also wondered if all this excitement would translate into a more active sex life at home. Her relations with James were still satisfactory, but had become a little routine.

The concrete floor of the office car park was dimly lit and not terribly well maintained. Novella was pleased she'd elected to wear flats today because in her state she'd have dropped a stiletto in one of these cracks in the first few steps. They approached his car and the lights flashed silently. He walked over to her side and reached past her. She could smell his cologne and her breath caught as she wondered what he was doing. He opened her door and gestured for her to climb in, and she stifled a giggle at her own over-reaction. He closed the door behind her and she placed her purse in the foot well and lay her jacket across her knees.

He climbed into the driver's seat and started the engine. Resting his arm on the back of her seat, he reversed out of the spot and paused to look at her. She felt like he had his arm around her and his open body language made her want to maneuver herself into the space he'd created. "Where to?"

Novella raised her eyes from his chest to his face. "Hm?" she questioned, snapping back to the present. "Oh! Where do I live?"

"You'll have to tell me, hun. I have no idea."

"Oh, no I meant. Never mind. Chatswood. Head towards Chatswood."

He took his arm off the back of her seat and she felt like another moment had ended. "Did you have a good night?" he asked, as they headed up the on-ramp onto the freeway. He was demonstrably sober enough to drive but the beer had given him a layer of good cheer and he was feeling buoyed by the repartee.

"Yes, that was a lot of fun," she said with a big smile. "So many cool people at this company! I hope Lesley survives her skydiving this weekend."

"Me too. Have you ever done it?"

"No. I'd love to, though." She looked down. "I've got quite a few things on my bucket list still, actually."

"Well don't leave them too long, will you. Life's short and all that crap."

"It doesn't feel short, and I think that's the problem. It doesn't feel like it's slipping away that fast, then all of a sudden you wake up and you're thirty-two and you've squandered the last ten years on work."

"I'm sure you had a life outside of work in that time, though." He glanced over at her. "But I know what you mean. A nine to five isn't terribly satisfying, and it's not much consolation when you're revising a bucket list."

He indicated to exit the freeway and they headed down the ramp into the outside of Chatswood. "Now where?"

"Stay on the main street." She indicated forward. "And when you get to the end, hang a right."

He nodded and she continued the topic. "The thing is, if I get sick or, heaven forbid, am in some kind of accident, you'll replace me. The company doesn't fold if I don't show up one day. But if I die having never seen the Maldives, or the gothic architecture in Europe, I will be really pissed!"

"Well I wouldn't replace you straight away," he said. "There would be a brief mourning period first."

She raised her eyebrows at him. He kept his eyes on the road. "Just a brief one?"

"A brief one," he repeated. "Then we'd go through the recruitment process and I'd keep comparing all the candidates to you, and they'd keep coming up short because your efficiency is out of this world."

A grin began spreading across Novella's face.

"And then when we discussed the scope of the job, I'd keep thinking back to how you schedule my appointments so that I'm never going back and forth between locations and I'd get so choked up."

Novella was laughing out loud by now.

"And then our staff turnover rate would quadruple in a year because no one could ever match up to your level of organization and I'd have to keep sacking them."

Novella pushed him on the shoulder. "Oh, stop it."

"And then my constant dismissal of PAs would eventually garner a grievance and I'd be advised that if I didn't get my PTSD from your death under control –"

" –PTSD?! Oh my god. You're such an idiot," Novella continued laughing through his deliberately preposterous predictions.

"But I wouldn't be able to because you always ordered the right brand of coffee and the projector always works when you've set up the meeting room for me." He had to raise his voice at this point to be heard over Novella's hysterics. "And the end of the story is that I end up committed and, in fact, the company does fold. So please, please don't get in any accidents. Or quit."

Novella pulled down the sun visor to access the makeup mirror and wiped smeared mascara away from under her eyes from where she had been crying from the laughter. "Oh my god. You're such a goose!" she exclaimed. "Okay, okay. I get the point. I'm indispensable." She put the mirror away and sniffed.

"Indispensable is the right word." He smiled and turned right at the end of the road, as instructed. "Ok, now where?"

"Take this left, and I'm the green house about halfway down. There it is." She gestured and he pulled over. The car was shaded by a tree that blocked Novella's view of the house. She wondered if James was still up. "Thank you for the ride."

"It was my pleasure. Allow me to complete the service." He got out of the car and jogged around to open her door. She wondered for a second if he'd stuck to his four beer limit: this was some unexpectedly chivalrous behavior. While he came around she tried to undo her seatbelt but the clasp was stuck.

She pushed her jacket onto the floor so that she could wriggle around and get a better look at it. It was the type with the button at the top that had to be depressed. She pushed down hard with both thumbs but it wouldn't move. He opened the door. "M'lady." He gestured for her to exit with a slightly wobbly curtsy. Those beers must have been right on the limit.

"It's stuck." She winced at him apologetically.

"What's stuck?" He let the door go and moved in to see what she was doing.

"It's the seatbelt. I'm supposed to push it down, right?"

"Oh, that one is always stiff. Lean back for a second." He reached across her and grabbed the buckle. Novella put both hands down the side of the seat nervously. The side of his ribcage was pressed against her while he fiddled with the clasp. His cologne was delicious; he smelled like sandalwood mixed with caramel.

"Sorry. I just have to. If you just push it in a little."

Novella giggled.

He smiled. "Don't be juvenile."

"Are we going to need scissors?"

"No, I can get it; it's done this before."

"Oh, I see. So, you know it's broken and you let me sit in the front seat anyway?"

He stopped wrenching the buckle and lifted his head. His face was about six inches from her own. "It's not broken," he said patiently. "It's just sticky."

"Oh." Novella didn't breathe. "Do you need a hand? I feel like I'm not being very helpful."

"You're right." He nodded. "You're making my life decidedly difficult right now."

"Sorry about that," she whispered. She could barely hear anything over the thudding of her own heartbeat. The tension in the eye contact was killing her, but she'd never enjoyed an awkward silence so much. About eight seconds passed before he kissed her. At the moment of contact, Novella's mind went completely blank. Both her hands came up involuntarily and cupped his face.

He let go of the seatbelt and turned his body to face hers, resting his hands gently on the sides of her waist. They stayed like that for a little while, each expecting the other to pull away. When the kiss came to a natural end, she opened her eyes and left her hands on his face, gently stroking the short whiskers with her thumbs. He smiled, sheepishly. "Didn't intend for that to happen."

"No," she replied breathlessly. "This is definitely the full valet service."

He laughed and kissed her on the forehead. "Should probably continue trying to get you out of this thing."

"That is a very good idea." Her hands were shaking and she felt like she was slurring from the wine and the pheromones.

He gave the clasp a massive shove and it finally gave, sticking down into its new position of properly broken. "Okay, you're free." He stepped back, giving her space to get out of the car. She retrieved her things from the foot well and shook out her jacket before swinging her legs sideways and hopping down out of the SUV. She stepped up onto the curb and turned to face him. "Thanks again for the ride home."

"Anytime," he said seriously.

Her brain was too scrambled to carry on any kind of witty back and forth, so she took a step backwards to break the energy field and said, "See you Monday."

He nodded. "Goodnight Novella."

•   •   •   •

James was sitting on the sofa drawing layouts of two different intersections about a ten minute drive from Elodie's house, when Novella came in. He hadn't decided which location afforded the best skid/roll room in the event that he struck her on the wrong angle. He lay the maps side by side and assessed the space, making notes on his pros and cons lists that included the likely traffic levels and height of the curbs. Though he was reasonably comfortable that his excited brain remembered the details of the two options accurately, he decided to do another reconnaissance mission to the locations before making a final decision.

"Hey. How was your night?"

He looked up from his notes and smiled. "Good. You?"

"Yeah, great. Listen, I'm so tired. I'm going to head upstairs and grab a shower before bed. See you up there?"

James smiled and added a line to the side of a drawing. "I'll be up in a bit. Just doing a little planning for work. Car stuff, y'know."

"Ok, honey."

Trawling potential locations for Elodie's demise had been positively delightful. He savored the process of choosing a time and drafting endless possible outcomes to ensure he'd covered his bases no matter how badly the collision played out. The plan was coming together and he was so lost in the detail that it was well after two in the morning by the time he went upstairs to bed.

CHAPTER EIGHT

James was parked on the north side of Abernathy Street wearing a foam neck brace and dark sunglasses. He'd chosen the last spot before a driveway and a fire hydrant so that no-one could park directly in front of him. He wanted to be able to swing out easily as soon as he saw her approaching. The hill was reasonably steep and made him feel like payload, sitting patiently in the bucket of a catapult, just waiting to launch himself towards his target.

The intersection he'd selected was quiet and the lights changed colors on a slow rotation. He'd arrived a half hour early to get a feel for the traffic flow before he had to be alert for Elodie. His stomach was in knots, but mentally he was ecstatic. His weary nervous system could sense the impending relief of having what amounted to an emotional tumor finally removed. Like having a bullet extracted, he anticipated some pain and tenderness to follow, but ultimately peace, as the wound finally closed.

He'd pulled over on the right, far enough up the street that he had sufficient time to build up speed. He presumed he had some wiggle-room with the speed limit; cops wouldn't be able to tell the difference if he was a measly ten miles over, especially since there weren't going to be any skid marks. He was going to ignore the red light completely and T-bone her clean off the road.

Whenever he imagined the accident he spent about a minute lamenting the fact that it would look too suspicious if his car was reinforced. As a mechanic, he had plenty of connections for roll cages and protective gear, but it was going to be bad enough when the cops realized his connection to Isabelle, without him being spotted wearing a full-face crash helmet in a lackluster sedan in quiet suburbia. He was already taking a lot of chances with this plan. He would be going as fast as he thought possible without incurring a reckless driving charge.

He looked at his phone. Ten minutes to go. He was already on high alert. He'd been monitoring her schedule for the past two weeks and, depending on traffic, her timing did fluctuate. He was staring intently at the top of the hill where he expected Elodie's car to appear when a tap on the window startled him. He snapped to attention so fast he was glad of the neck brace.

An elderly man with wispy white hair and deep eye bags was pressed up against the window with a curious expression.

"Yes?" James snapped, leaving the window up.

"Good afternoon," the old man began questioningly. "Saw you sitting outside my house for a while, thought I'd come out and see if you were broken down?"

"No, I'm fine." James tried to maintain a polite tone. "I'm just sending a text message, then I'll be on my way." He held up his phone to indicate what he meant. *Please know what a text message is*, he thought to himself. He cast his eyes back to the road and scanned for Elodie's BMW. Nothing yet. The idea that she might have come through while he was distracted was intensely stressful.

The old man didn't move. "What are you doing with the phone? Is your car okay? I can call someone if you like."

"What the fuck," James whispered, fumbling for the window button. The glass began sliding down before the old man had moved his face back and the unexpected movement knocked him off balance. He grabbed at the door to steady himself as the window slowly opened. "I'm just sending a message to my friend." James enunciated clearly, pointing to his phone at each word and punctuating the sentence with desperate glances at the road Elodie was due to be on at any second. "I will be gone soon."

"Were you looking for someone on this street?" continued the old man, demonstrably missing the point of James' explanation. At that exact moment, James caught sight of Elodie's car in the distance, making its way toward the intersection. He looked at the traffic lights. His was orange, meaning hers was about to turn green. At that distance, with no traffic in front of her she wouldn't be stopping. This was it. He had to go. "Sorry, sir," he shouted at the old man. "I have to go. Have a nice day."

The old man's eyes narrowed at James' dark glasses and obvious agitation.

Elodie's BMW continued towards the lights. It was time to launch.

He started putting the window up, pushing the old man's hands back off the car. "Hey!" He stumbled backwards onto the footpath. "Sorry, sir. Gotta go!" James tried to apologize;

he was acutely aware that making people in this neighborhood suspicious wasn't helping him and now he was likely to have a witness. Fuck, fuck, fuck.

Hurling the phone into the passenger's seat, he turned the keys in the ignition, rammed it into first gear and dropped the clutch. He peeled away from the curb, cursing the fact that he'd probably left tire marks behind. James' hair blew into his eyes; he shoved it out of the way in between violent gear changes. He was up to third and doing a decent click as he approached the intersection. Elodie's car was ahead of him. She was going to make it. "NO! NO! NO!" James shouted, gripping the steering wheel and planting the accelerator, completely forgetting the part of his plan where he wasn't speeding when he hit her.

Elodie sailed through the intersection, her eyes on the road ahead. James hit the intersection doing approximately thirty miles over the speed limit and missed the back of her car by about six feet. He let out a guttural cry of defeat as he careened into the quiet residential street opposite, pumping the brakes in a panic.

He managed to get the car to come to a full stop a couple hundred yards down the road. Pulling up to the curb, he took the car out of gear but didn't turn it off. He smacked his head against the headrest a couple of times and let out a shaky sob. The disappointment was visceral and it made his skin burn. He wanted to cry for hours, but his pattern was to take sadness and make it anger. So, he did. He coughed out the last sob and swallowed the tears. He punched the steering wheel a couple of times and the dry, cracked vinyl on the old steering wheel cut the skin on his knuckles. He yanked the neck brace off and put the bleeding part of his fist in his mouth.

He thought back to the old man he'd left standing and confused on the side of the road. He'd taken a good look at James' face and made it fairly clear that he thought he was lurking. He would remember him, so if there was to be another attempt it would have to be at a different location. The idea of trying this again made James so very tired. The adrenaline pump, the excitement, and the mammoth anti-climax had absolutely drained him. God, what if there had been someone right behind her? He could've T-boned the wrong car. He could've killed the wrong person. The reality of just how wrong this plan could have gone hit him all at once and he sat, unmoving, in the car for a few minutes.

He wasn't going to attempt this again. But she still had to go. Only it wouldn't be vehicular manslaughter. His intense agitation triggered his compulsion. He needed a burn. What a shame Elodie Doucet didn't hang out in empty factories at night. Two birds, one stone. His eyes widened with sudden realization.

The idea came as if heaven-sent. It materialized, fully formed in the center of James' consciousness like a gift from a higher power. It played out like a movie projected on the windscreen of his car as he sat watching, receiving, and processing the inspiration.

If Muhammad won't come to the mountain, he thought, *then I will have to bring the mountain to Muhammad.*

• • • •

Novella weaved, elbowed, and stepped carefully around the other patrons in her favorite bar, dexterously maneuvering a tray of mojitos and sambuca shots back to the pod of women waiting expectantly in a corner booth of The Havana Club. It was 'Thirsty Thursday' and she was enjoying a little cocktail-assisted girl time with Bianca and Megan, her two best friends, and two of Bianca's colleagues who were new to the city and looking to find a social group.

Bianca was an approval-junkie, so when she overheard Zara and Alina talking about how difficult it had been to break into a social circle, she immediately inserted herself into the conversation and sold them on Thursdays at Havana. The bar had recently been refurbished and was, realistically, as modern and clean as you could get whilst remaining reasonably priced. Happy Hour was two-for-one on certain cocktails and Novella had downloaded a handful of Free Shot coupons from their website so it was a very affordable night out.

Novella slid the tray of drinks carefully onto the table to a chorus of squeals and clapping. The shots were clinked and sunk first. Bianca's colleagues had already been introduced with a brief bio and an enthusiastic round of one-downsmanship:

"Your dress is gorgeous!"

"No, your top is the *best*! What a great color on you!"

"Your highlights are *to die for*. What salon do you go to?"

"Oh no, it's just a good toning shampoo. Your bangs are *perfection*!"

Once the rejection of compliments and the first round of drinks was out of the way, the conversation moved into more personal topics. Zara had moved to the city after a relationship breakup had acrimoniously divided the couple's friend group. She had decided the best way to get over her ex-boyfriend was to get under someone else, which suited Megan. Both of them had been scanning the room for potential targets since they got in the door and were in the process of bonding over their shared love of the chase, while simultaneously lamenting their low date-to-boyfriend conversion rates.

"Do you usually have much luck in here?" asked Zara, taking a big draw on her mojito and stabbing the remaining ice cubes around to encourage melting and create more drink.

Megan squinted in thought. "I don't do too badly. Good weeks and bad weeks."

Novella tried to hold her facial expression steady. Megan's 'good weeks' inevitably turned into 'bad weekends' for Novella when Megan ended up either on the floor of her bathroom with borderline alcohol poisoning or on her doorstep in tears after yet another catastrophic failure. She loved the night out, the cheap drinks, and the girl talk, but Megan was requiring greater levels of supervision and she was starting to wonder whether she would have to dish out a little tough love in the near future.

"Is this the right place to be meeting people. though?" Novella asked, trying to sound genuinely interested.

Megan and Zara looked at each other. Zara laughed a little as she responded, "Where else do you meet guys?"

"Well," Novella stacked a few coasters and tried to choose her words carefully, "Don't you think you'd have more luck if you tried talking to guys who were out doing things you liked to do? Then at least you'd know you had something in common with them, and you'd have seen them clear-headed and in the full light of day, so no nasty surprises the morning after." She took a sip of her drink and tried hard not to let her eyes dart to Megan.

Megan looked slightly affronted anyway. "I don't have 'nasty surprises,' thank you very much. I just sometimes think I 'set the bar a little low,' is all"

Novella almost gave herself a cramp trying not to let her facial muscles show what an understatement she felt that to be. "I just think, when you meet someone in a bar, you can't really be sure that you are compatible, because the lights are dim and the conversation is limited and we've all had a bit to drink, so obviously the rapport is somewhat lubricated."

Megan's brow began to furrow again.

This wasn't going as well as Novella had hoped. She tried a different tack. "You like to go to those personal development seminars, Megan. Have you tried pulling there?"

Megan looked at her like she'd suggested intentionally contracting leprosy. "Um... No? The lights are up, we're all sober and talking about our baggage. I don't think that's the best place to try and sell myself. Besides, I go to those when I'm struggling and I usually wear my glasses instead of contacts. I'm not in pick-up mode at ten a.m. in a conference hall."

"Oh god, no. That'd be awful," Zara chimed in. "Besides – cleavage." She gave hers a prod to signify its importance.

"Here, here," said Megan, lifting her glass to salute the succinct point, and looking down quickly to make sure hers were still pushed up to her collarbones and blanketed in highlighter.

"Have you tried speed-dating?" asked Alina, quietly. Even this early in the conversation everyone could tell she was going to need at least two more shots to get friendly.

"I did! About six months ago." Bianca waved her hand, excited to be an authority on something. "So, I didn't really want to go but another friend of mine didn't want to go alone so I was roped in."

Megan rolled her eyes, obviously unconvinced that there was any arm-twisting required.

"I think it's absolutely worth trying, assuming you're not too shy to start random conversations, but because there's a limited time with each person you have to be prepared to get some dealbreaker questions up front."

"Oh, god. I can only imagine." Alina's eyes widened.

Bianca shuffled in her seat, getting comfortable for her favorite story. "One guy sat down in front of me, didn't even introduce himself, just opened with, "Do you want kids?" I just started laughing. I said, "Right now? You offering?" Not a word of a lie, he didn't even crack a smile. He literally repeated, "Do you want kids? At all? Ever?""

The table grimaced in unison as the divisive topic was thrown out.

"I said that I hadn't started planning that far ahead, but that I assumed I would with the right person at the right time and he totally shut me down. He actually said "I'm out. Do you want to make small talk, or check your phone until the timer goes?""

Bianca's audience reeled back in a mixture of incredulity and amusement. A cacophony of 'oohs' and 'whoas' and 'no ways' filled the air around them and attracted the attention of the nearest five or so tables.

Megan said, "I want to hear more of those, but I think we're going to need more drinks for this." She got up and made a beeline for the bar.

Novella watched her with a practiced eye. Because of Megan's volatile relationship with men and alcohol, she had become somewhat hyper-vigilant on these nights out and subtly attempted to manage Megan's alcohol intake. Two drinks in and she was still doing fine; a rosy glow and slightly increased volume. Three rounds from now, she'd be unable to get herself to the bar and back.

The bar was warming up from all the increased traffic and Novella's legs were starting to sweat against the cheap vinyl of the newly upholstered booth seats. She tugged her skirt down to provide a barrier and tried to engage Alina in the conversation. "How's your love-life going?"

"It's pretty quiet." Alina was looking down but a small smile was curling the right side of her lips.

"Pretty quiet, my ass," interjected Zara. "She's got her eye on one of the project managers at work."

"That doesn't constitute a 'love life'," Alina defended quickly. "That just means I hope next time you ask I'll have a different answer."

"Sounds pretty promising!" Novella nodded supportively. "What's his story?"

Alina's eyes lit up at the chance to talk about her crush. "Well he's great, his situation is a bit iffy though. He's tall, good looking, surfs." She waited for the inevitable nods of approval before continuing. "But recently divorced, sees his five-year-old on the weekends."

"Oh yeah, that's tough," Novella said with a grimace. "Was it an amicable split?"

"Not really. But it's civil, now."

"As long as he's not still grieving the ex, I think she should go for it." Zara swiftly steered the conversation back to light-hearted.

"Oh absolutely – and I am going to try." Alina was enthusiastic. "We had lunch last week and we didn't get back to the office for nearly two hours!"

Novella let out an involuntary chortle at the mention of the long lunch, thinking back to her conversation with Mr. McRae in his car. Two sets of raised eyebrows were about to question her reaction when Megan arrived back with another tray of drinks, and another round of shots. Novella stifled a sigh, noticing that Megan had switched to gin. "Bottoms up, ladies!" Five shot glasses clinked, and there was a second of silence, before a chorus of "Eurgh! What was that?"

Megan laughed. "Fireball – cinnamon flavored whiskey. My favorite!"

The fact that Megan was mixing liquors did not bode well. Novella desperately wanted to say something along the lines of "Let's slow it down," or "Shall we have some water?" but she wasn't sitting close enough to Megan to do it surreptitiously and there was etiquette around masterful handling of spiteful or sensitive drunks. A process, if you will.

The shot glasses were returned to the tray and only Megan licked her fingers; the other three wiped the pungent liquor on bar napkins and rinsed their palates with mojitos. "I think you have to go back for another round," Zara chastised. "I chugged half my drink swilling out that chai-scented jet fuel."

"Good." Megan took a big gulp of her gin and tonic with extra lemon. The smell of gin always reminded Novella of methylated spirits and grass clippings and her bathroom at 3am on a Sunday, so she was pleased to be a good distance away from it.

Megan stood up. "We need to get this party started anyway."

"Easy there, Gatsby," said Novella, before she could stop herself. Halfway through the second drink and two shots down had put a vibrant flush in her cheeks and she could feel herself wanting to make a night of it. In the past, she'd have simply gone to work hung-over with a quad-shot liter o'latte in each hand, but she didn't want to be puffy-eyed in front of Mr. McRae. She looked at her watch; it was only seven thirty. Still plenty of time to enjoy the buzz and then sleep it off.

Megan raised her eyebrows at the 'Gatsby' comment but didn't get a chance to make anything of it, before Novella continued with Alina.

"So, what did you talk about on the long lunch? Do you two have much in common? Do you think he's sweet on you, too?"

Alina blushed, looking up through her long eyelashes at Novella. "I think so. I mean, I don't like to talk myself up but the body language was pretty positive. Lots of smiling, lots of flattery, lots of eye contact. We definitely connected." She played with her hands as she spoke, clearly hopeful about the potential suitor and self-conscious about her evident emotional investment.

The women fawned over her in a tipsy display of affectionate encouragement. Zara returned the question. "What about you, Novella? What's your situation?"

"Oh, she's married." Megan said, waving a dismissive hand. Only Novella recognized the envy behind the derisive tone.

"Yep, nothing to see here." Novella held up her left hand so the women could see her modest wedding set.

"Well it's not really nothing, is it?" Megan said. "It's a symbol of how much someone loves you and wants to be with you forever."

There was an awkward silence as the other women realized Megan's gin was likely going down the wrong way.

"I didn't mean the rings, Megan," Novella said patiently. "I meant in reference to my love life. No juicy tales of office romances or one night stands here." She smiled and hoped Megan would feel the others' discomfort enough to take a back seat for a bit. But it was not to be.

"Well, not yet anyway." Megan smirked and finished her gin.

Novella grimaced at the size of the swig and bit: "What do you mean by that?"

The others sat silent, watching the interaction intently and barely brave enough to take a sip of their drinks, lest they break the rising tension.

"Nothing." Megan shrugged. "Just remembering you telling me how hot your new boss was and thinking how nice it must be for people who have so many options." She put the glass down on the table firmly and pursed her lips in a challenge. *A real shame she didn't have anyone to cry over at the moment*, thought Novella disdainfully. *That gin's staging a sit-in at Angry Town.* To be brutally honest, she preferred tears. Just as embarrassing, but less combative.

A kitchen-hand stopped by the table and collected their empty glasses. Bianca smiled at them in thanks, but didn't say anything for fear of interrupting Novella's reply.

"My boss is not an 'option'. I told you he was hot because you asked me how my interview went, and easy questions from a good-looking man makes for a pretty decent job interview, if you ask me." She winked at the three spectators who remained enthralled by the exchange. It was obvious there was history to this and Zara and Alina in particular felt privileged to have struck drama pay dirt on the first outing. They both knew they'd be angling for Thirsty Thursday invites again, and they smiled widely in response to the wink.

Novella continued, "I really don't appreciate you using benign, throw-away comments to embarrass me when we're trying to have a fun night out. Are you going to perk up, or do we have to order some food and a pitcher of water to get us back on track?"

Megan's eyes narrowed. "We were never 'off' track."

Novella's calm tone made her appear even more confrontational. "There's no need to be dramatic. We're all having a great time." She gestured at the others, who immediately raised their drinks, now mostly melted ice from having been held and ignored for the duration. "Whose round is it?"

Zara immediately raised her hand. "I'm up!" She shimmied out of the booth and paused when Novella grabbed her arm softly. "Get some fries and a garlic bread while you're there, will you?" Zara nodded and smiled knowingly. Novella straightened her shirt where it was gaping a little in the front and finished her drink.

Megan's attitude was cringe-worthy enough without her deliberately, publicly, insinuating that Novella was hot for her boss. A low blow, and Novella felt distinctly uncomfortable with people knowing that there was anything (no matter how small) between her and Mr. McRae.

She made a mental note that Megan wasn't going to be one of 'those friends' anymore. No more 'girl chat,' no more confiding. And she might need to lay off being the default couch and counselor every other weekend. She couldn't be sure of what Megan would say these days, and lines like tonight's were not at all welcome anywhere near James. Megan's emotional decline, and the fact that it seemed to be taking their friendship with it, saddened her.

But she had bigger issues to deal with right now. Like the fact that the mere mention of her boss' name had made her decidedly uncomfortable in an amorous and inappropriate way. She hoped James was still awake when she got home so that she could burn off a little of the energy.

CHAPTER NINE

James stopped at the workshop on the way home to drop off the tools he'd borrowed. When he pulled into the car park he was alarmed to see a police cruiser outside the building, and one uniformed and one plain-clothes officer talking to Jeff in the doorway of the office. Both had short brown hair, cut military style. As he got out of the car, Jeff looked over at him with recognition and relief. The officers turned to follow his gaze and immediately began strolling towards the car.

"James Tallon?" one of them called out as they approached.

"That's me," James said, his stomach starting to churn. He thought running a red light only got you a ticket in the mail. *Please God, tell me no one phoned in my license plate.*

The officer in plain clothes held up a name badge and introduced himself as Detective Jensen, and his uniformed friend as Officer Stewart. "Do you know anything about the Eastside Autos warehouse on the corner of Cranbrook and Frewin Street?"

James' breath caught in his throat. They were asking about his last burn. "Um," he tried to look nonplussed, but he could only manage blank. "It's, um... It's a warehouse... Where they store imported cars." His voice was shaking.

"Well, it was," said the detective, keeping eye contact. "Someone tried to burn it down a little while ago." Both policemen watched his reaction intently.

"Oh wow, really?" James tried to look shocked but he knew his reaction times were slow and his body language was wooden from anxiety. "Is it... okay?"

"Okay?" The detective looked at the officer quizzically before continuing. "No it's not 'okay,' Mr. Tallon. It was gutted."

"Oh no." James shifted his weight to the other foot and tried to appear casual, but he knew he looked like a marionette doll with several key strings missing. He desperately wanted to know where this was going. If they'd already pinged him he should be in handcuffs by now. He waited for them to volunteer something.

The policemen subtly exchanged raised eyebrows. Detective Jensen continued, "The reason we're here, Mr. Tallon, is that your fingerprints were found on the exterior door."

James' brain fizzed at the inconsistency. "How were my fingerprints found anywhere if someone burned it down?" he said.

"I didn't say it was burned down – I said they *tried*," he replied. The detective's eyes had widened at James' sudden clarity. "It was gutted. We ran all the prints from what we could salvage of the exterior and you popped up. Care to tell us why?"

A pregnant pause followed as James' brain imitated a laptop with a blocked fan. His prints were in the database from an assault charge after Isabelle's death. He'd gotten into a bar-fight, but been convicted and discharged as his lawyer had successfully argued provocation and asked for leniency given the recent bereavement. He could feel himself perspiring with the effort of finding the right answer. Suddenly the file he wanted appeared.

"I used to work there," he said. "Jeff probably told you already." James gestured in the direction of the office, but Jeff had retreated inside. "We do contract work out there – certifications – when they get a large shipment and they're overloaded." James elected not to go into any further detail. He was pretty sure his voice was still shaking and he was fighting hard to come across unruffled.

Both policemen looked visibly disappointed at the dull, yet credible story. They paused for a moment to see if he would offer any more detail for them to qualify, but James held his ground and waited for them to accept his explanation.

Eventually, Officer Stewart broke the silence with a reluctant acceptance. "Okay, Mr. Tallon. We have your contact details from your boss already, so we'll likely be in touch once we've verified your comments and made some more progress with the investigation." He gave a fake smile. "Be sure to let us know if you're leaving town at any time, won't you?"

"No problem." James nodded and started walking towards his car. The officers watched him take the bag of tools he'd borrowed out of the back seat and carry them into the workshop.

Inside, he put them all back in their designated spots and walked over to where Jeff was on a creeper under a black Honda Accord. He kicked his shoe. "Hey."

Jeff slid out and looked up at James. "What's the deal with the Auto warehouse? Someone burned it down?"

"Yeah, they just wanted to ask me about it because they found my prints there, but I said they'd be left over from the last certification job we did."

"That was months ago. You reckon they'd still be there?"

James blinked a couple of times before responding. "Well they must be, Jeff," he said slowly, in a tolerant monotone. "Because they found them." His jaw was tight. "How else could they have gotten there?"

Jeff looked confused and James, still tense from the questioning, gave up. "Don't worry about it. It'll be fine. Are we still on for that early start tomorrow?"

Jeff looked pleased to be back on a topic he was totally across. "Absolutely. See you then." His trolley wheels squeaked as he rolled back under the car. James stood for a moment, watching Jeff's greasy sneakers loll about. The skeptical look on the detective's face stayed with him. He had the distinctly uncomfortable feeling that wouldn't be the last time they spoke.

• • • •

Outside the Brake n' Lube, Detective Jensen was sitting in the passenger seat of Officer Stewart's patrol car, eating a selection of lunch items out of a Tupperware container his wife had packed for him. Officer Stewart was acting as chauffeur while Jensen's car was in the shop and thoroughly enjoyed accompanying him, as he hoped to one day be a detective himself. Jensen gestured thoughtfully towards the building with an asparagus roll and looked over at Stewart. "You buy it?"

Stewart tipped his head to the left and grimaced like Christopher Walken. "I don't know. It's just boring enough to be legit, and yet." He took a deep breath. "Something about him wasn't right. For such a boring response, why so fidgety? Why was he hopping around so much? If you know the warehouse because you occasionally work there, why be all shaky and strange about it?"

"Perhaps we're just that intimidating," replied Jensen, eyeing his fruit kebab with annoyance. There was a gross grape blocking the pineapple. He looked around. There wasn't anyone watching. He considered firing it out the window. "Yeah, I didn't like him either. He may not have done the warehouse, but he's definitely doing something illegal."

"Do you want a car outside his house?" asked Stewart. He was wondering if there was any actual coffee underneath the takeaway cup of foam he'd picked up on the way over. Jensen watched him carefully replace the cup's lid and lick a bitter coffee-ring off the inside of his thumb before he bothered to respond.

"No, not yet." Jensen narrowed his eyes. "I might keep an eye on this one myself for a while."

• • • •

"Elodie, I feel like we've lost momentum."

Dr. Goulding had taken his glasses off and was sitting forward, with his elbows resting on his knees, no longer able to hide his exasperation. "Do you want to make progress, or do you want to spend the rest of your life panicking about people from your past? Because right now I'm not feeling any desire on your part to either manage or heal your anxiety. What do you want to achieve with these sessions?"

Elodie struggled to form a reply. On the one hand, she was uncomfortable questioning Dr. Goulding because of his position of authority and his propensity to speak firmly in a way that intimidated her, but on the other hand she firmly believed her fears were valid. She didn't see how they could make progress on her anxiety as long as the fact remained that she'd been responsible for a death, but never held legally or morally accountable. Why couldn't he see that her guilt was real, and normal and healthy? It meant she had a conscience! Why didn't he understand that they weren't addressing the core of the problem?

She said, "You keep asking me to do exercises, like reliving the event dissociated, like a spectator, to make it smaller or less painful in my head," she began, tentatively, "but I don't want to make it smaller. I don't deserve for it to be less painful." Her voice broke.

She took a deep breath and swallowed before continuing. "You don't understand. You want me to stop fixating on it but she lives in my head. You want me to recognize that I can't control her family's pain but I am the very cause of it! They won't forgive me. She doesn't forgive me."

"She's *dead*, Elodie!" Dr. Goulding exclaimed, clearly vexed by her dedication to this broken record.

Elodie's eyes welled up.

Dr. Goulding closed his eyes and sighed. "Elodie, there are a lot of exercises and techniques we can use to help you, but if you don't want to be helped then we may have taken this as far as we can go."

"What do you mean?" said Elodie, sniffing back tears. There was confusion in her eyes, but her fear of abandonment had already been triggered. Her breathing grew shallow.

"I can tell we're not making any progress," he said carefully, "because you don't do any of the exercises we prescribe, and you're still using your maiden name to sign in. I have noticed you expect the receptionists to address you as Ms. Doucet. I think in your head you are still 'on the run.' Would you agree?"

"No." Elodie's tone was petulant. She refused to make eye contact. "I use my maiden name because there are often people in the waiting room with me and it's none of their goddamn business who I am or why I'm in a therapist's office." Her brow was furrowed. "Are you saying I'm a lost cause?"

"No," said the doctor, patiently. "I'm saying treatment will only work for you if you want it. If you are determined to stay in this victim loop then the therapy can't possibly work, because it requires your participation and effort."

"I'm not a victim!" Elodie shot back, indignant. She sat up straight for the first time since she'd arrived. "That's the whole fucking point – I'm the perpetrator! I'm the murderer!" Dr. Goulding tried to get her attention. His tone was low and he enunciated each word carefully. "Elodie. No one is trying to say that you didn't commit the crime. Track with me here. I am listening to you. I have heard what you said. What is missing is your willingness to move forward. Do you understand?"

"Oh, I understand," she said, with a hostile tone. She stood up quickly and wobbled a little on her heels. "Believe me, I'm not the one who doesn't understand." She picked up her purse and checked that her phone, wallet, and keys were all there.

Dr. Goulding watched her, resigned. "How would you feel about seeing a different therapist?"

Elodie shot him a venomous stare. "Fuck you." She collected her coat from the arm of the couch on her way to the door. She yanked it open and didn't close it behind her, storming straight through reception without a word. As she marched, she could hear Dr. Goulding's instructions to his secretary. "Claire, can you please send Mrs. McRae's files to Dr. Fife at Central Medical, and then also a letter to her home advising future appointments with me have been cancelled."

•   •   •   •

The photocopier was being recalcitrant. Novella re-set it for the fourth time and put the hand-outs back in the top tray. She was exhausted and exhilarated. Ever since Mr. McRae had kissed her in his car, the tension in the office had been agonizing. Barely keeping afloat in a sea of innuendo, she struggled to keep on top of her tasks and there were a few close-calls with the scheduling. Unsurprisingly, Mr. McRae was lenient and forgiving in his response.

Her increased attention to her personal appearance had thankfully (and if she was honest, a little disappointingly) not generated any concern from James. Her new motto was 'If I can put a blazer over it, it's work-wear,' and the broad scope of application this allowed her meant several dresses usually reserved for nights out had made it into the office. Mr. McRae's appreciative glances didn't go unnoticed and Novella was elated every time she caught him staring, or her outfit triggered a flirtatious comment.

Because he had his own office, she was able to meet her ever-increasing need for contact by standing too close when she was taking him through documents or getting signatures. The glass front prevented them from actually embracing, but the frosted panel across the middle meant that occasionally, when he was brave enough, he could put his arm around her hips and hold her close to him while they worked.

The infatuation had struck her at an opportune time. Novella still loved James, but she was no longer 'in love' with him. She was bored in the bedroom and James' preoccupation of late made her feel lonely. As though he was aware of her presence, but only in bursts and only when pushed. She felt that he made assumptions about her place in the relationship as dutiful wife and dinner-generator and, deep down, she wanted to shake those up. Just because she married him didn't mean she wouldn't like to feel impressed, or special, or irresistible ever again.

The conversations she had with her boss throughout the day were filled with humor and double entendres. Witticisms and scarcely concealed flattery. Private jokes and irreverence. And the temptation was simply too great. They were going to have to do something to break the tension. Like rain clouds relieving the humidity of a week-long build-up of cloying heat, the storm was definitely coming.

"Are those hand-outs ready?" He was standing behind her. They were alone in the office and he was inappropriately, gloriously close.

"Almost. The copier keeps showing the error screen, so I'm only getting two out per re-set." She could smell his cologne and she didn't give a rat's behind about the hand-outs. "I'll probably be another ten minutes. Are you ready to go?"

"Ready and willing," he replied. "Did you block out both calendars? I don't want to come back to a bunch of post-it notes and shitty voicemails."

"Yep, both of us until three." They were heading across town for a meeting with a major client. Mr. McRae was giving a presentation and Novella wasn't sure why she was going, as their admin would be able to handle the technical side, but he said he needed her and that was all the convincing that was necessary.

"Make it four, will you? This is likely to run over."

Novella finished battling the copier, put the handouts in a folder, and amended the calendars. They met downstairs in the car park at eleven thirty and drove to the client's office on the other side of town. Due to the timing, the meeting was catered and Novella enjoyed listening to the presentation and eating free sandwiches. She tried not to swoon visibly every time Mr. McRae fielded a question with impressive intellect and detail, or negated a smugly delivered criticism.

Twice the client's receptionist crept in quietly and topped up everyone's coffee cups from a fresh pot. Novella felt a little out of place, sitting in the back of the room and not actively contributing, but the young woman smiled sweetly at her anyway and even brought her vanilla flavored cream from another part of the office as a welcoming gesture. Novella was briefly embarrassed by the extra attention, but accepted the favor graciously.

The presentation ended smoothly after an hour. Novella was devastated – she was obviously happy to watch him strolling around the end of the boardroom being authoritative and intelligent and smelling delicious for as long as he was happy to do that, but if the presentation was only an hour, were they seriously going to do more than three hours of questions? She bit into another sandwich, looking deflated. She honestly didn't care what any of these people had to say; she just wanted to get back in the car, drive to a suburb where no one knew them and make out.

He asked for questions. A gentleman in the back, wearing the ugliest tie Novella had ever seen, questioned the proposed timeframe. It was agreed that it was optimistic, but not unachievable. The call went out for other questions, and the client representatives looked at each other, agreed they'd seen enough and stood up to leave. While Mr. McRae was shaking hands and volunteering Novella to email all parties various project information, she was celebrating, and imagining what would happen once they were back in the car.

She helped him pack up the left-over paperwork and they walked out to his car. "Well you overshot that one!" Novella laughed.

"Overshot it? How so?"

"You said it would run until four. It's not even one thirty."

"Well, look at that," he said, climbing into the driver's seat and reaching between them to put the paperwork on the back seat. She watched him get organized, thinking how nice it would be to just lean into the space he created by reaching. She wanted to, every time he put his hand on her seat to reverse. But they were still in a public car park. Much too risky.

Before he started the car, he said, "Whatever will we do for the next two hours before we need to head back to the office?"

He was looking directly at her. Her stomach turned over. "I don't know," she started nervously. "What would you like to do?"

"Novella, can I be honest with you for a second?"

"Absolutely."

"I don't think this is sustainable."

Her heart sank. She tried not to let it show on her face, but the disappointment must have radiated out of her at warp speed because he hurried to clarify. "What I mean is, I can't deal with this tension anymore. I need to hold you."

Novella couldn't control the size of her smile. She knew she was showing too many teeth and her crow's feet must be taking up half of her face, but she was so damn excited, and flattered, and provoked. "Okay," she managed.

"So how do you feel about a little detour on the way back to the office?" He started the engine.

"To where?"

"A hotel?"

Novella was suddenly terrified and exhilarated all at once. She desperately wanted to climb this man, but she'd never done anything like this. And a hotel room was awfully real. The wave of euphoria around their connection had carried her these past few weeks and simultaneously soaked away most of her guilt for two reasons. She deserved to be happy, she told herself, and she hadn't actually slept with him. If they went to a hotel room now, there was no turning back. If she went with him now, she was having an affair. The battle raged inside her head, but both sides ultimately knew who would win. The logical, practical married woman was going to concede to the overwhelming chemical storm swirling in the dark blue SUV.

"A hotel?" she repeated.

"A hotel," he said, pulling out of the client's car park. "I booked one."

Her eyes widened. "Presumptuous?!"

"I don't think so." He grinned. "I feel like it would have been incredibly naïve of me to think this wasn't going to have to be dealt with."

"*This*? What is *this*?"

"*This*, my dear." He put his hand on her leg as he drove. "Is a foregone conclusion."

He drove to the other side of town and pulled into a small, boutique Bed n' Breakfast. There was room to drive around the back and park the car out of sight, which she assumed was intentional. He undid his seatbelt and opened the door but she didn't move.

"You coming?" He looked concerned that she may have changed her mind.

"I don't need to check in with you, do I? Can I wait in the car while you do the paperwork?"

He laughed. "You think I would march both of us into reception in the middle of the day and ask for a room just like that?

I already have the key, Novella." He smiled patiently and she unclipped the newly repaired seatbelt and climbed down, holding her bag nervously. He unlocked the door and held it for her. She walked in and put her things down on a beautiful timber dressing table next to a very plush looking super-king bed.

Before she had time to panic and say something awkward, she felt his hands grasp the collar of her jacket and slide it down her arms. He threw it on the chair and stepped around to face her, his arm already around her waist, pulling her into him as he buried his fingers in her hair and kissed her. The room disappeared.

She unbuttoned his shirt roughly, tearing the bottom ones off in her haste. He unzipped the back of her dress and pulled it down; he seemed desperate to feel her bare skin against his chest. It was deliberately skintight and clung to her hips. He slid his hand down the inside, refusing to let her go as he helped her wriggle out of it. With her lips on his neck he walked her over to the bed. She felt the cool linen against the back of her legs and lifted them, one at a time, to wrap around his waist. He knelt on the bed with his right arm supporting her as she kissed him, moving from his mouth to his neck and back again, alternately savoring the sweet scent of his cologne and the taste of his mouth.

He pushed the display cushions off the bed with his left hand and pulled the pillows into the center. He set her down on the bed, her head and shoulders sinking into the cloud of Egyptian cotton, and lowered himself onto her. She loved the weight of him; he was so much taller and broader than she was and she felt enveloped by him. For a brief second, she thought of James. He was lighter, leaner, less crushing.

The memory was uncomfortable and she didn't stay with it long enough to really register the guilt; there was too much urgency. Their hands moved over each other, exploring and mentally recording positive reactions to revisit later, but not pausing anywhere yet. He wanted to know every part of her intimately; she was enthralled by every curve of his chest, every ridge on his abdomen.

The pressure that had been building up over the past few weeks finally found an outlet in the form of feverish gripping and insatiable teasing. She loved the way he held her against him and moved her body around as though she were weightless. She could tell he adored the feminine curve of her tiny waist by the way he held her as she arched back in ecstasy. They came together with her on top of him. She collapsed onto his chest and buried her face in his neck, exhausted and shaking. He was euphoric, but shocked.

"I've never done that before," he gasped.

"I doubt that," she murmured, confused, but too spent to converse properly.

"Ha." He was breathless. "I mean, we...at the same time. That's never happened to me before."

She smiled. "Felt good though, huh."

He closed his arms around her and kissed her forehead. She remembered back to when he'd done that in his car. It was a charming habit.

"I hope you like this hotel room," he mused, quietly.

"Yeah, it's nice," she replied, running her hand up his side, clearly disinterested in the location.

"Because I think I might lease it," he continued with a wry smile.

She laughed. "You think we'll be back?"

"Oh, there's no way we're not doing that again." He shook his head, resolute.

She smiled. She was beatific. They canoodled for a little longer, before the time constraint of the workday forced them to get up and re-dress. She helped him with his shirt buttons and apologized for the two that had been torn off. He zipped up her dress, slowly, taking the time to fawn over her lingerie and kiss the back of her neck as he went.

Leaving the hotel room was torture. Separating to each get into their respective car seats was like dragging magnets apart and they reconnected the minute they were inside, his hand on her leg and her arm reaching up to caress the back of his neck as he drove them back to the office. About a block from their building they reluctantly took their hands back. Novella double-checked her makeup and hair in the visor mirror, then reached over to adjust his tie and smile at how beautiful he was.

CHAPTER TEN

James' alarm was unbearably loud; he despised both the alarm itself and its necessity. He slept through melodies and listened to radio alarms without moving. Anything less than a harsh plastic speaker imitating a seagull caught in a six-pack yoke didn't cut the mustard. He stabbed at it blindly, trying to stop the audio strike before Novella got angry. She'd come home late from work last night and looked pretty wrung out so he knew she wouldn't appreciate being included in his five o'clock start. His flailing hand eventually found the correct button and the onslaught stopped. Groggy, sitting up in the dark, he rubbed his eyes and pushed his hair off his face. It needed a cut.

It took a couple deep breaths to get him off the bed and into the shower. He regretted volunteering for the early start, but, realistically, he couldn't have avoided it. He was currently the only employee Jeff could afford and these cars had to go out. He turned the shower dial to a cool temperature and pulled the lever out all the way, hoping the maximum pressure would go some way toward waking him up. He'd had a terrible sleep, full of angry people, accident scenes and wild goose chases, and he was very much looking forward to coffee.

As he stepped toward the shower he caught a glimpse of his reflection in the mirror above the sink. The dark circles under his eyes were shockingly deep. He leaned toward the reflection and pressed at the dull skin of his face, noticing for the first time that the stress was aging him more visibly than he had realized. Elodie was taking up too much space in his system. Between the residual pain of discovering her life was flourishing while his deteriorated, and how much mental energy he was giving to planning her death, he felt like a shell of his former self. He stepped into the shower, putting his face directly under the jet of water in the hopes that it would stimulate some kind of circulation. He needed blood flow and a decent moisturizer, stat.

The memory of seeing the police officers outside his work appeared, bringing with it a dull nausea. He had broken his routine and was paying for it. Always two reconnaissance missions in the week prior to understand the human traffic patterns of the location. Make a list of requirements and check off every item in advance. No rushing, no preoccupation, and certainly no last-minute decisions before the burn. That's how mistakes get made. That's how cops end up finding your fingerprints at the scene of the crime.

He was losing it.

The prospect of prison terrified him. His name was on a police file for an arson attack. An old man near Elodie's suburb probably had his license plate down in case anyone asked him about hoodlums in the area. He'd become much too extroverted for someone with his proclivities.

There was no more room for spurious accidents with elaborate set-ups and he was acutely aware of how tight to his chest he needed to play his cards from now on. He needed to get away from being so emotional about Elodie and back to the rational, calculated premeditator he had been with his fires.

As he soaped and rinsed under the stream of cool water, his final plan was coalescing. Since he couldn't get Elodie into an accident, he was going to have to bring an 'accident' to Elodie. He shampooed his hair slowly, mentally stepping through the fuels and components he'd need, the time it would take, and even the clothes he would wear. The rhythm and order of list-making busied and focused him. Some of these tasks could be completed tonight, he realized with excitement, as Novella was working late again so he was free to come and go with suspicious looking items.

He finished in the shower, toweled off, and put on his work clothes. Downstairs the coffee pot was full and steaming, thanks to him setting the timer the night before. He filled his thermos to the brim and sealed it, fishing a lid that doubled as a cup out of the dish-rack.

Lastly, he rummaged around in the back of the pantry for some granola bars to get him through the morning at work, but could only find cranberry flavor. He really preferred the apricot ones. He toyed with the idea of taking them anyway, but remembered they were Novella's favorite. Better leave them for her, he thought, throwing the box back haphazardly.

He would pick something up from the bakery on Ninth. He loved that place. Picturing the cabinets of custard squares, fresh croissants and various cakes made his mouth water. Suddenly he stopped. Cakes. Celebrations. He looked at the date on his phone. He and Novella had missed their anniversary. His heart sank.

He'd been so preoccupied with stupid Elodie that the day had come and gone and he'd not said a word. James stood for a moment, leaning against the pantry and looking at the date on his phone screen with genuine remorse. He needed to make it up to her one night when she wasn't going to be working late. He decided he would cook her an elaborate dinner. Real effort on his part would show more contrition and love. She deserved so much more, but he couldn't allocate any more mental energy to celebrating until Elodie was dead.

$\bullet \quad \bullet \quad \bullet \quad \bullet$

Novella added sliced sourdough to the chopping board covered in olives, cheeses, and other delicious antipasti and carried it over to the bed in their small hotel room. "Afternoon tea is served," she exclaimed proudly, her mouth watering. He poured two glasses of wine and handed one across to her. They clinked glasses and each took a sip.

It was four-thirty on a Thursday and they had left the office early under the pretense of a client meeting, driven straight to a hotel and immediately torn each other's clothes off. Exhausted and famished from their love-making, they devoured the entire platter, dipping anything solid in anything less solid than that, and coating everything in the herb-infused oil of the marinated artichokes.

"I don't know why you insist on putting your lingerie back on," he teased, pulling her bra strap off her shoulder playfully. She laughed through a mouthful of bruschetta and put the strap back. When she could speak, she replied, "I don't like walking around hotel rooms naked. I always feel like anyone could just walk in at any moment. Besides, these were expensive. I want to get my money's worth."

They were in continuous contact. He stroked her bare legs as they ate, she played with his fingers as they talked. As soon as the food was gone, they immediately drifted back together and lay down on the bed. She curled up against him and rested her head inside his shoulder. He reached down and pulled her knee up so that her leg lay across his hips.

She had been living from bliss bubble to bliss bubble the way many people live paycheck to paycheck. The elation of the payout, followed by the euphoria of having been 'replenished,' which barely lasted a day, followed by the crushing need for more. Between hotel rooms he metered out emergency provisions in the form of innuendo, miserly contact, and suggestive glances. Like a shopping addict obliterates their wages on unnecessary purchases, she was completely depleted of him and craving his touch within twenty-four hours of being separated. The euphoria of their connection was tempered by the debilitating lows of their separation.

As they lay together in the bed, drinking each other in and becoming inebriated by the pheromones, the silence grew heavy with all the things they wanted to say. He started. "I want to see you more. I need to see you more."

She squeezed him around the ribs. "I know what you mean. The time in between hotel rooms is torture."

"Torture!" he agreed with enthusiasm, lifting himself off the bed and rolling over to stroke her hair. He looked into her eyes earnestly. "What's the next step?"

She ran her hands over his shoulders, feeling the warm skin and tracing the indentations from the end of his collarbone over the shoulder muscles and down his arm. "I don't know," she said honestly, thinking of James. "We're not single."

"I don't think that's a good enough reason to miss out on this," he said stubbornly. He pushed a stray hair away from her eyes. "I knew from the moment I saw you sitting outside my office that I was in trouble." He smiled, his eyes gentle.

She smiled back.

"And I don't feel like it's one-sided." There was no intonation at the end of his sentence, but she knew it was a question.

"It's absolutely not one-sided," she replied, incredulous that he would even suggest it. "But it's not a black and white situation."

"Absolutely. But I think you're worth whatever drama we have to navigate."

"Same." She smiled a bittersweet smile. "We have some difficult conversations ahead."

"I'll do mine if you do yours."

He held her eyes for a few moments before leaning forward slowly and pressing his lips to hers. She returned the kiss, enjoying the immediacy with which he pressed the rest of him against her. He found her hands and lifted them above her head, pressing them down into the plush pillows with his right hand, while his left moved under her to unclip her bra. With the clasp released, the underwire lifted and he slid his hand under the lace cup and over her breast. A small moan escaped her lips as his fingers grazed her nipple and he moved to kiss her neck. She lifted her legs to wrap around his waist.

Lost in the heat of the moment, he couldn't keep it in any longer. "I love you, Novella." He said earnestly, his mouth just beneath her ear.

She replied without hesitation. "I love you too, Damian."

• • • •

As James drove up to his house, he noticed one of the neighbors' children had left their bicycle on his curb, forcing him to swing out wide before pulling into the driveway. He stepped out of the driver's seat, with his arms full of fresh vegetables, wine, and cake for a belated anniversary dinner, and kicked the car door shut. Bags in both hands, he balanced the cake box on his forearms, and stepped cautiously towards the door. He was paused on the front step, wondering how to get the key into the lock, when he heard footsteps behind him.

"Need a hand?"

James looked over his shoulder, unwilling to spin around completely lest the cake take an ungraceful swan-dive onto the concrete pathway.

"Oh, hi Megan." He tried to keep the disappointment out of his voice. "That'd be great, thanks. Are you looking for Novella? She's not home yet."

"Oh that's okay. I can wait." She held the cake while James unlocked the door. He stood to one side and gestured for her to go in first. She smiled and led them up the corridor and into the kitchen, walking stiffly in platform boots and exceptionally tight jeans. She placed the cake box carefully on the counter and opened the lid. "Oh, it's gorgeous! How decadent. Is it a surprise for Novella?"

"Uh, yeah." He came around the counter and closed the lid before putting the cake away in the fridge. "Thanks for helping with that," he said, trying to temper his briskness. "I'm not expecting Novella home for a while. She's working pretty long hours these days."

Megan's eyebrows went up. "You don't say."

She perched on one of the barstools and James looked slightly confused that Novella's absence hadn't triggered her exit. "Whatcha making?" She eyed the grocery bags. "Special occasion?"

Megan was the last person James wanted to talk to about having forgotten his and Novella's anniversary. "Sort of. Can I get you something to drink?" He was offering more from the need to change the subject than any desire to encourage her to stay and talk.

"Sure. If there's a bottle of wine open, I'll take a glass." She pulled some pilling off the front of her top, flicked it away and began combing her fingers through the ends of her hair, which were thin and knotted easily thanks to the bleaching.

James plucked a half-finished bottle of pinot noir out of the wine rack and poured two deliberately stingy glasses. May as well have some too, he thought. He was cooking Italian, after all.

"Is everything okay with Novella?"

James took a big sniff of his glass to make sure it was still drinkable. He wasn't sure when the bottle was opened but there was no hint of the tell-tale vinegar scent. "I assume so?" he responded, before taking a sip. He liked pinot noir; he liked how fruity it was. The taste of dark cherry and plums reminded him of his grandmother's homemade jam.

Megan waited a few seconds to see if he would take the bait, but his face was expressionless. She tried again. "Only, I was out with her the other night and she seemed... a little off. Kind of tense, you know?"

"She's been working a lot. Maybe she was just tired."

"Yes, she has been working some pretty long hours, hasn't she?" Megan's point got a foothold. "I mean, I'm sure she enjoys it. She *really* likes her colleagues." She nodded earnestly, realizing James didn't do subtlety.

He missed the nuance. "She's probably more excited about the money. Now that we're back to two incomes we were hoping to take a vacation at some point."

"Oh, great! Going anywhere fun?"

"Not sure yet. Hopefully somewhere warm." James' brevity and lack of enthusiasm was making the conversation awkward. He and Megan had never really got on; he couldn't figure out why she was trying to be so social with him now. She was preening too, which was weird. He started putting groceries away.

"I'm so happy for Novella, with her new job and all," Megan continued. "My boss is a super-jerk, but she seems to be getting on *really* well with hers."

James was stacking cans in the back of the pantry to create more shelf space. "Is she?"

"I mean, I don't know much, but she said the interview was really friendly and like I always say, a bit of eye-candy around the office never hurt anyone." She took a sip of her wine, her eyes focused on the counter top.

"Eye-candy?" James stopped unpacking and picked up his wine glass.

Megan giggled, suddenly nonchalant. "Oh, you know what I mean. Her boss is a bit of a babe, is all. I'm secretly hoping she can hook me up!"

James didn't laugh. He'd always found Megan desperate and this wasn't helping that perception. "Ok, cool. Good luck with that."

They both drained their wine glasses. Megan stood up. "Okay, well. I suppose I better go. Thanks for the drink."

James followed her down the corridor, noticing molted strands of hair clinging to the back of her top. He wondered if he should suggest to her that she get the waistband on her jeans let out, as it was creating a sort of 'popped sausage' effect around her middle. He decided to stick with, "I'll tell Novella you stopped by." He threw her a forced smile as he stepped into the doorway to keep her moving.

"Oh no, that's ok. I'll text her later." Megan waved away his offer, stepping quickly down onto the path. "Don't worry about it. Have a great dinner."

He watched her cross the street but closed the front door before she got into her car. Her comment about Novella's boss made him uncomfortable. He didn't want to talk to Megan about her conquests, potential or otherwise. He was surprised at the idea of Novella acting as matchmaker, though. She'd always encouraged Megan to back off when it came to guys, to focus on her own life under the assumption that the right man would show up once she was happy with herself and doing what she loved.

But what Megan loves is chasing guys, thought James, scoffing. He remembered the last time he caught a glimpse of her upside down on his bathroom tiles, her hair full of regurgitated gin and her eye makeup everywhere but her eyes. He poured himself another glass of wine and took a chopping board out of the cupboard. He had a lot to do before Novella got home.

• • • •

Elodie had been home for over two hours, pacing and neurotically wiping down surfaces, when Damian walked in. He was nervous to see her sitting on the couch with a purposeful expression; she'd obviously heard his car in the driveway. He'd planned to slink in quickly and get to a shower before she wanted to talk. He had done the best he could with his appearance, but he knew he was more rumpled than when he left the house that morning.

His jubilant mood, courtesy of Novella, dissipated as soon as Elodie stood up and started walking toward him. As she approached, Damian could see she'd been crying. He braced himself for the emotional tornado he knew was coming.

"You're awfully late tonight," she said.

"That's why they pay me the big bucks," he said, fatigued. "Are you okay? You look like you've been crying."

"It was a rough day, actually. Nice of you to ask. Would've been nicer if you'd actually been here, but I guess I'll settle for a cursory enquiry."

Damian sighed. "I don't choose my work hours, Elodie. If you needed me, you could've called." He put his jacket and briefcase down on the counter, resigned to the fact that he wasn't going to get upstairs for a shower. "What happened?"

Elodie walked into the kitchen and scoured the wine rack for a shiraz. "You'll be pleased to hear," she said, still choosing, "that Dr. Goulding let me go."

"He let you go?" Damian said, quizzically. "Can they do that?" He was genuinely confused. He'd always assumed the client decided when they left.

"Evidently!" she said, impatience and condescension dripping from every syllable. She poured the shiraz into a glass and took a large gulp.

"Did you two have an argument?"

She smirked. "It was less of an argument, more an attack."

"By who?" Damian pictured Elodie's sixty-something, chubby psychologist punching her in the face and resisted the urge to laugh.

"By him, obviously! Why would I attack anyone?"

Damian let her question hang in the air for a second, wondering if she might pick up on the irony that she had launched what felt like an attack the minute he came in. She looked expectantly at him, waiting for a reply. He gave up and moved the conversation on. "I don't know, Elodie. What did he say?"

She took another mouthful of wine and looked past him for a minute. He could see from her expression that she was busy deciding how to relay the story with as much malice on the part of the therapist as possible, to ensure her victim-status remained intact. She clicked her tongue, while she thought about how best to explain. He could see her deciding what details best corroborated her outrage. "He *accused* me," she began, with theatrical emphasis, "of not wanting to get any better. As though I actually enjoy having anxiety. Who the fuck would enjoy anxiety?"

Damian correctly assumed the question was rhetorical and stayed silent.

"Then he said that I should see another therapist." She looked down after saying that. Damian could see she was hurt by the perceived rejection. He wanted to tell her that Dr. Goulding was likely recognizing that he couldn't take her any further, rather than making a statement about her personally, but he sensed it wouldn't do much good.

"Did he have anyone in mind?" Damian ventured. Elodie shot him a malevolent stare. "Anyone that he thought might be better suited to you?" he clarified. "Does he want you to try a different style of therapy? Did he make any recommendations?"

"I don't fucking know what he wants." Elodie was sullen.

"I thought he was giving you exercises?" Damian continued. His experience was screaming at him to shut up and let it go, because these types of conversations never ended well. But after the day he'd had with Novella, he was less inclined than usual to put up with this shit. Suddenly the consequences of actually giving her free rein seemed less ominous.

Maybe she screamed her lungs out and he slept on the couch. Fine by him. Maybe she called him every name under the sun and he stormed out and got a hotel for the night. Bonanza! He'd send Novella a text message in case she could sneak out, too. He was already going to have a have a much more difficult conversation with Elodie in the very near future anyway, may as well drive a wedge first.

For the first time since Elodie's anxiety reared its ugly head, Damian didn't feel as though he was on eggshells. He felt decidedly courageous.

"He *was* giving me exercises."

"And?"

"And they don't work!"

"They work for other people though, don't they? That's why they're the official exercises that therapists prescribe." Damian was feeling confident now.

"What do you mean by that?"

"I mean, that the exercises aren't arbitrary. They are being prescribed for a reason. Did you discuss with him why they don't work for *you*?" Damian decided he could use a drink too and made his way to the liquor cabinet.

"Yes, of course we discussed why they don't work for *me*," she mimicked. His meaning was not lost on her and she looked resentful at his dubiousness. Damian finished making a gin and tonic and took a sip while he waited for her to elaborate. She looked at him and he waved his hand, indicating that she had the floor.

"Well, he thought it was because I wasn't participating fully, which was bullshit." She looked all around the room as she spoke, and Damian could tell she was picking and choosing what she reported. She was holding onto her wine glass firmly and was already halfway through it.

"How did you show you were participating fully?" Damian asked calmly.

"How did I show it? By doing the exercises, obviously."

"Then I don't really understand the problem, Elodie. Can you give me any more details?" He took a sip of his drink without dropping her gaze.

"Well, it's obviously more complicated than that," she snapped, exasperated. She could tell he was being deliberately obtuse and the attempt at mollification bothered her. It felt like he viewed her upset the same way he would a three-year-old having a tantrum. He didn't understand the seriousness of the situation. A voice in the back of her head reminded her: *he can't understand. He doesn't know what happened.*

She dismissed the temptation to throw some truth into the mix. While her ego loved the shock value and the sympathy that usually followed her outbursts, she was fairly sure that this was one she and Damian wouldn't be able to come back from.

"Enlighten me," he continued.

His relaxed demeanor was getting under her skin. This wasn't the way their fights normally went. "It doesn't matter."

"The fuck it doesn't," he announced. "If I'm paying for these sessions, then I would like to know that you're getting some value out of them. And if you're not, then I would like to know why."

"And there it is." She nodded, her lips curled into a sneer. "The big man lays out the big money for his highly-strung burden of a wife and when she's not fixed like that – " she snapped her fingers, " – he wants to know where his hard-earned cash went." She looked up at him, defiant. "You want to know where it went? It went fucking nowhere. That's where it went. Because no over-priced prick in a fancy office with a big sofa and a big certificate can fix what I have."

"What do you have?" asked Damian.

"GUILT!" she shrieked. "Crushing, debilitating, brain-fogging, skin-burning, all-consuming guilt!" Her eyes were wet with unshed tears. She couldn't stop herself.

Damian didn't react to her hysteria. "Guilt over what?" His unaffected demeanor irked her somewhere deep.

"I killed someone," she said, quietly.

CHAPTER ELEVEN

Damian felt as though his lungs were turning to cold clay. His face flushed and he was suddenly short of air. The silence was palpable. "What?"

She stared at him, serious.

"When?" he asked, not entirely sure he wanted to know.

"Ten years ago. I hit her car with mine. On purpose. It spun off the road, rolled, and burst into flames. She was burnt alive." Elodie finished her wine. "That's why the therapy isn't getting rid of my 'anxiety.' Because it's not fucking anxiety. It's the monstrous, crippling guilt of knowing one of my temper tantrums put someone in the ground."

Damian swirled what was left of his drink around and around in the tumbler. He watched the lemon slice shed flesh, broken down by the alcohol, into his drink. He swallowed the last of the G&T in one gulp, feeling the friable slivers of lemon catch on his tongue on the way down.

"Get out," he said.

Her eyes widened. "Excuse me?"

"You heard me." There was no discernible emotion in his voice. "Pack a bag and get out. You can go stay with your mother. I'll have whatever you can't carry right now shipped and the house stuff can be dealt with via our lawyers." He wandered over to the liquor cabinet and began to make another G&T.

Elodie was shocked. "Damian, I..."

"I'm done, Elodie." He turned to face her, holding a fresh drink. "We're done." He stepped around the coffee table, sat down on the sofa with his back to her, and tasted his drink. He winced a little; he'd poured it pretty strong.

She sat, stunned, on a barstool at the kitchen counter, her fingers still wrapped around the stem of her long-empty wine glass. "You piece of shit."

He ignored her.

She reached forward and smacked the pile of junk-mail and various subscriptions across the dining room floor. Several hard-spine car magazines slid across the carpet and hit the skirting boards, coming to rest in and around the floor-length curtains.

Damian said nothing.

The silence was deafening, so Elodie broke it by hurling her wine glass against the wall with a guttural scream. "YOU FUCKING BASTARD!" she shrieked. "YOU HEARTLESS PIECE OF SHIT!" She lunged at the couch where he was sitting.

He was up and out of the way by the time she reached him. She came at him fists flying, but at a solid foot taller than her, Damian had both the strength and size advantage. He grabbed her by the wrists, wrenched her arms down by her sides and shoved her down hard onto the armchair.

He knew from a previous incident that there was no room for gentleness once she'd crossed the physical line. He hoped none of the neighbors were looking through their windows. She was still shouting obscenities, so he stepped over the arm of the chair and crushed her newly-restrained hands with his knee, freeing up one hand to cover her mouth. She tried to bite him and he pushed her head back against the headrest roughly. "Calm. Down," he said, through gritted teeth.

She struggled against his weight and he could hear her trying to scream in the back of her throat, so he leaned more heavily and she eventually softened. Her eyes welled up. He took his hand away from her mouth and she coughed. Damian shifted his weight to his right leg and stood up, releasing her wrists. She continued to cry as she rubbed at her bruised hands.

"Please don't call the police," she said, her voice small.

He stood next to her, watching her with pity. If he was completely honest, most of his love for her had been eroded over the past six months, so the majority of what he was feeling in this moment was exhaustion. "I don't particularly want to involve the police either, Elodie. So, here's what you're going to do to ensure we avoid that. You're going to go upstairs, and pack a bag. Then you're going to drive to your mother's and tell her you'll be staying for a while. Anything else you want to say to me can be said through our lawyers. Understand?"

Elodie nodded and wiped away her tears with the sleeve of her top. She stood up and walked past him, shaking. In fifteen minutes, she had filled a gym bag with essentials and was ready to go. When she came out to the lounge, she was saddened to see him sitting on the sofa, staring into space with red eyes.

"Damian?" She half expected him to see her to the door. "I'm sorry I didn't tell you before."

He didn't move. "Me, too."

She turned and left, fresh tears erupting as soon as she closed the door behind her.

• • • •

James took the cake box out of the fridge and tore it open so that he could slide the ornate, ganache-filled monstrosity carefully onto a pretty platter. He was going to bring it out after dinner as a surprise. He wondered for a second if the fridge was a secure enough hiding place, but it couldn't really go anywhere else. The kitchen was warm and he didn't want the cream parts to collapse. To be safe, he re-arranged the alphabet fridge magnets to spell out 'NO GO ZONE.'

Smiling at his own creativity, he emptied out the grocery bags and began preparing dinner. He was making pasta primavera with a marinara sauce. Simple, but delicious if you had time to slow cook it. He had finished the chopping and was scrubbing onion scent out of the wooden cutting board when Novella arrived home. He was glad she was late because he had intended to take his time with the dinner.

James had been looking forward to both the food and the look of gleeful surprise he expected to see on her face when she realized what he'd done. The house was fragrant with onion, garlic, and thyme sautéing in the pan when she walked into the kitchen to see James splashing about in the sink and smiling in her direction. "Hey, baby." He grinned. "How was your day?"

He was determined to be as loving and benevolent as he could to counter the potential negativity that might pop up around the real anniversary being forgotten. He was contrite about missing it and was ready to field any criticism or hurt. He dried his hands and came out from behind the island, extending his arms toward her.

In what he registered as an uncharacteristic reaction, she didn't move forward into his embrace. She just stood there, holding a few shopping bags, waiting for him to slowly cross the dining room floor. He gave her a welcoming kiss and a hug which she participated in dutifully, but with little conviction.

He put it down to post-workday fatigue and returned to the stove-top to stir the sautéing vegetables. "Are you hungry?" He continued with zeal, attempting to carry the energy along for both of them.

"Yeah, I suppose," she said, thoughtfully, putting the bags down carefully and taking a seat on one of the barstools.

James pushed a rebellious piece of onion off a hotspot before it burned and smiled at Novella resting her elbows on the bench with a pained and weary expression.

He misread her silence as residual displeasure at the missed anniversary and sought to console her by introducing the evening.

"James," she began, carefully.

"No, no." He smiled. "Let me start."

She silenced her sigh of resignation and gestured for him to begin.

"I want to open with an apology. I know I missed our anniversary, and I am really, really sorry for that, babe."

Her face fell.

"So," he said, pausing for effect. "I would like to make it up to you tonight." He pushed the finely diced vegetables around the pan a little more before pouring a tall jar of crushed tomatoes over it and waited for a response. She looked a bit shocked at the idea that there was a planned, possibly romantic, event imminent, but wasn't smiling.

He reached back into his arsenal. "Also, I bought you a present." He indicated the dining room table where a small box with a perfect gold bow sat up proudly, on her favorite placemat at her usual seat. Novella's head moved slowly from James, to the gift and back again. She still wasn't smiling, but now her eyes were a little wider and looked wet. He couldn't tell if she was still upset, or overwhelmed by the gestures. He really wished she'd say something.

He decided to play his last trump card. He opened the fridge and lifted the cake out, resplendent on the floral platter they'd received as a wedding gift. It was a black forest gateau with whipped cream decorations, finished with glazed strawberries. Novella gasped.

"Can you pass me a glass of water, please?" she said.

A little bewildered, he set the cake down and reached up into the cupboard for a glass, rinsing it under the tap before filling it and passing it across to her. She drank heartily, trying to swallow the lump in her throat.

James watched her silently, slowly stirring the marinara sauce and trying to decipher where he'd gone wrong.

"Thank you for the gift," she said, finally, "and the dinner, and the cake." She smiled and pressed the outside of her eyes with her thumbs, pre-emptively catching tears before they could carry her eye makeup down her face.

James felt nervous. "You're very welcome, but you don't look terribly pleased about any of it. I am *really* sorry about missing our anniversary, honey." He chewed on the inside of his cheek while he watched her expressions and waited to find out how bad the damage was.

"It's ok," she said, truthfully.

"But it's not," he pushed. "You're clearly upset."

She laughed, but it wasn't a joyous sound. "I'm not upset because you forgot our anniversary, James. We both forgot it."

James' confusion heightened. "You forgot, too?" He was at once relieved, and a little hurt. "So why are you so upset? Doesn't that mean I'm only half as much in the dog-house as I thought I was?"

She nodded.

"So, what are you crying about?" He turned the stove down and came around to where she was sitting to put his arms around her. The embrace wasn't welcomed and James could feel her discomfort.

"I'm crying because we need to talk. We need to have a serious talk, and it's not going to be fun." She pressed her eyes to the sleeve of her shirt to soak up the tears that had freshly welled. "I'm crying because the sight of that platter reminded me of our wedding, which makes this conversation all the more difficult."

James' stomach turned over. He didn't know what she was talking about, but he was pretty sure he didn't want to hear it.

"Our relationship has been flat-lining for some time now," she began, unable to make eye contact. "And I think we need to see it for what it is."

"What... it is?" His head was enveloped in a creeping cold, but strangely his ears were hot. This usually only happened when he'd drunk too much. He wondered if he might vomit.

"We had a good time together." Novella pushed her fingers back, one by one, causing the joints to click. It was a nervous habit and she did it most often when she wasn't enjoying someone's gaze. "But I think it's come to a natural end. We're basically roommates. I still care about you, but the passion is gone. The 'in-love' part is gone. I know you feel that, too. We almost never talk anymore. I've come home from work late almost every night for weeks now and you haven't even asked why my hours have almost doubled."

"Why have they doubled?" asked James, numbly.

Novella immediately regretted using that as an example. She hadn't wanted to bring Damian into this discussion. She brushed it off. "We have a new client and they're really demanding. But that's not the point. If our marriage was still on fire you would've asked; you would've noticed."

"On fire?" He thought that an odd choice of words. "Novella, people's marriages don't stay 'on fire' twenty-four seven.

Relationships can be work. There are ups and downs. We've only been married for four years, for Christ's sake."

"I get that." She didn't want to argue the point. She'd run this emotional gauntlet in her own head and she didn't want to go back through it. She was completely besotted with Damian and that level of euphoria had shown her a type of love she simply couldn't generate with James. It was intoxicating, and spectacular, and she wouldn't give it up.

"We need to separate." Her tone was final, but she still couldn't make eye contact.

James looked at her, incredulous, his mouth open to speak but no words came. After a couple of choking coughs, he managed to splutter, "You're breaking up with me?" He started heaving from the effort it was taking not to cry. He put his hand on the countertop to steady himself and looked around frantically.

Novella didn't know what to do. Her first instinct was to go and help him but she wasn't sure how. She also didn't want to breach this newly formed barrier and risk giving him any sense of hope through physical contact. She stood up. "Breathe, James."

He looked in her direction when she spoke, but she wasn't a hundred per cent sure he saw her.

"Why... Where did this even come from?" he asked.

"We've been separated for a long time, James. We just kept living together, pretending everything was okay. Let's be real for a second. You don't even notice when I'm not here!" She threw her hands up in exasperation.

"What do you mean I 'didn't notice' you weren't here?" he asked, his eyes screwed up with genuine confusion. "You said you were at work. I assumed you were at work. Where is this even coming from? You start working longer hours and suddenly I'm the one who's checked out?" James' mind was whirring. He'd had blinders on this entire time. He'd never questioned her work hours because... because why? His brain frantically searched for a reason. Because why would she lie? Because working longer hours is a good thing; it means more money for their holiday and why would she turn that down?

But she was right. He hadn't just missed her work hours, he'd missed her. His mind flashed back to that fateful day when he first saw Elodie walking across the street outside the pub. The weeks since then had been a blur of anger, of fixating, of plotting and planning, of ruminating, of burning, of sneaking around, punctuated with one beautiful interlude where Novella had met him at the door in red satin lingerie and they'd enjoyed a wonderful, passionate night together.

She had put in so much effort, he realized with a horrible skulking guilt, and what had he done? Enjoyed her, and then immediately gone back to his fixation on Elodie. Was it still an emotional affair if you utterly loathed the person you were 'seeing?' His ears were still hot. Affair or no, he had barely said two words to Novella for weeks, maybe months.

You don't even notice when I'm not here, she'd said. And she was right. Well, she was half right. He did notice she wasn't there, because he was pleased. He could work on his plans to kill Elodie in peace. "Novella, I'm so sorry," he said, his head tipped to the side with genuine contrition. "Please don't quit us. Let me make it up to you. Let me be here." He stood up straight and put his arms out, pleading.

He started walking towards her and she sidestepped him. "I've said my piece, James. It's too late for all of this. You need to accept that we're separating."

This was moving too fast for him. He'd gone from sautéing onions for homemade marinara to the brink of divorce in under an hour. "But I love you." He said, still refusing to cry.

"Thank you," she whispered.

He winced at her response. "I just..." He looked at his hands, still completely lost. "I just don't understand how we got here. I understand that I've neglected you and I'm so, so sorry for that. But, where is the talk? Where are the questions? Where is the fighting? We've just gone from what I thought was fine to... to now?" He tried to catch her gaze, but she was all over the room like a bored teenager in Sunday school. He couldn't shake the nagging feeling that he'd missed something.

She sighed. "Not everything has to be a dramatic meltdown," she admonished, "Sometimes adults just grow apart. We're on different paths. It sucks, it hurts, but it's the truth."

"No, fuck that." The red flag in the back of his brain was getting bigger. "There has to be more to it than that." Megan's awkward visit popped into his head. "Oh shit!" He suddenly realized he'd forgotten the sauce and leapt back to the kitchen to take it off the heat. It was a bit thick, but not ruined.

Novella watched him pour the sauce into a container without saying anything. Truthfully, she was starving, but it didn't seem appropriate to ask for the meal he'd been making for their belated anniversary dinner. She decided to pack a bag, and go get a meal and a hotel room.

It was at this time that James realized that the little red flag in the back of his mind had writing on it. Like the answer to a crossword puzzle, it had been right there this whole time, only he couldn't articulate it.

"You don't even notice when I'm not here."

Not "when I'm at work,", not "you don't care about what long hours I'm doing," not even "you don't even notice that I'm being over-worked."

"You don't even notice when I'm not here."

The bolt of truth was jarring. "You weren't at work," he said, bent over in front of the fridge, clearing space for the sauce he didn't want to eat.

"What?"

"You weren't at work, were you?" He turned and made eye contact with her.

"What do you mean?" she asked, nervously.

"You said that I didn't notice when you weren't here. But I never thought you 'weren't here.'" he explained, indicating the house. "I thought you were at work. But you weren't."

Novella swallowed, but didn't reply.

"Who is he?" He stood to face her.

"Who's who?" she said, weakly.

James brought his fist down on the kitchen counter so hard the container of utensils next to the stove jumped. Several tiny red spatters adorned the laminate.

"WHO. IS. HE?"

Novella was staring at his fist. *Please don't start hurling shit around*, she begged silently. "There is no he."

"Don't fucking lie to me." He was shaking his head. All the late nights she'd had over the past couple of months were popping up in his head like a montage; his brain was flipping through all the nice work outfits he'd noticed, but not complimented her on in the mornings. Suddenly, given the correct context, his brain was placing information morsels into their homes, like a half-finished jigsaw puzzle coming together to form a picture of his wife with another man. The conversation with Megan was a quiet soundtrack in the background.

Novella saw the glow of her phone silently receiving a message in her peripheral vision.

"How long has it been going on?"

Novella didn't want to participate in the inquisition. She picked up her handbag and walked towards the stairs. "I'm going to pack an over-night bag and go to a hotel. I think we should take some time to cool down."

"It's going to take more than one fucking night for me to calm down, Novella," he called to her as she made her way up to the bedroom. "I'm going to find him, and I'm going to gut him."

· · · ·

Upstairs, Novella took her phone out and opened the message from Damian.

Elodie's gone. We're done. Can you come over? xx

Her heart leapt. She quickly typed a message back:

On way. Love you xx

She dropped the phone back into her handbag and grabbed a suitcase out of the wardrobe. As she quickly selected her most loved and oft-worn items to take to Damian's house, she could hear James moving around downstairs. She wondered momentarily if he might come upstairs and try to stop her taking her things, but she needn't have worried. He was striding the length of the kitchen and dining room, back and forth on repeat.

Novella came downstairs to find James talking to himself, out loud, while pacing an invisible track up and down, looping the kitchen island and around the dining table. He was so involved in his own muttering that he wouldn't have noticed her leaving him, had she not been standing in the doorway agape, watching him with morbid fascination. The bright purple of her dress caught his eye. He looked from her, to her suitcase, and back up to her.

"I get that you need some space. I understand space. I know what that feels like." He rubbed his hands over his hair, scratching at the scalp before pushing it roughly out of his eyes. "But we're going to talk, right, after we've had the space?" His eyes were imploring and she was compelled to agree with his agitated nodding.

"Sure," she said, cautiously. "We can talk in a while."

"Okay. Okay, good. So, you're going to a hotel tonight?"

"Yeah." It was then that Novella noticed the tick. He was nodding so forcefully it was difficult to properly take in his expression but his left eye seemed to be catching on something. He started clapping as though he was excited to move forward on what they'd just decided. She was suddenly scared. This was a huge level up on his usual state of pre-occupation. She picked up the suitcase and walked towards the door, fighting the urge to bolt.

"I'm going to fix this, Novella," he called after her. "I know what I have to do."

She closed the door behind her and went to her car as fast as she could with the weight of the suitcase. As soon as she was behind the wheel she locked the doors, but James never came out. She could see him through the dining room window as she started the car, orating and gesturing like a lunatic.

CHAPTER TWELVE

Parked under an old oak tree down the street from James and Novella's home was Detective Jensen, incognito behind dark glasses and a black beanie, nursing a thermos of hot tea in a beat-up Mazda he'd borrowed from his teenage son. He'd been watching the interaction through the dining room window and was wondering if he would have to intervene, right up until Novella exited out the front door carrying a suitcase that looked to be of reasonable weight. Must have been a good fight, he thought, squinting into the binoculars. Even with prescription sunglasses his aging eyes still struggled with detail.

He put them down and looked away as she pulled out into the road, but resumed watching the house immediately in case James decided to follow her. Jensen was both concerned and a little entertained to see that James didn't appear to have properly registered the fact that his wife had packed and left. He continued to pace and talk and gesticulate in a noticeably energized fashion for a solid fifteen minutes as Detective Jensen peered up the driveway with a worried expression.

The guy was clearly having an episode. Jensen put the binoculars back in their case and weighed up his options. It was getting late and he had to get the car home so Miles could get to football practice. Furthermore, he didn't really want to have to confront James this early. He wasn't sure how much more personal surveillance he'd have to do to catch him in the act, and he didn't want him to tap a vein over his wife before he had the chance to break the law again. He pulled out his phone.

"Colleen? Jensen here. I need someone from Mental Health Services to do a house call. I have a suspect under surveillance who appears to be having a bit of a breakdown. I'm not in a position to approach at present."

He listened as they confirmed the details of the request and passed on the address. "Just have them say a neighbor phoned it in. The house has big windows; it's not too far-fetched to assume someone saw the domestic and the ensuing distress."

He gave Colleen a description of James and hung up the phone, squinting up the road with a concerned expression. Assured that someone was on the way, Detective Jensen drove home.

•   •   •   •

Elodie only managed to drive a couple of blocks away from the house before she had to pull over and collect her thoughts. She adjusted the rearview mirror to inspect her face, expecting her makeup to be a mess, and she was not disappointed. Her lipstick was smeared from Damian's hand and her mascara, diluted by tears, had congealed haphazardly, sticking her eyelashes together in clumps. Small spots of it clung to the skin beneath her lower lashes, topping off the long streaks that marred her formerly flawless foundation.

She pulled a tissue out of her handbag and wiped at the black spots roughly, before scrubbing the tear stains away. She tried to blend what was left of her foundation, but patches of her skin showed through.

The thought of driving to her mother's nauseated her on a good day; with her face a mess and her marriage in a similar state, she couldn't fathom dealing with condemnation and dismissal. She closed her eyes and took a few deep breaths as she contemplated what to do. Some of her friends lived close by, but none of her social relationships were developed or close enough that she felt comfortable just arriving on their doorstep.

She pulled out her phone and scrolled through the messages, looking for something recent. A declined invitation to a baby shower. Agreement to donate to a charitable initiative, but a regretful apology regarding the celebratory dinner. A request for more time to consider whether she wanted to chair a committee.

She made several attempts at jovial opening lines.

"Hi Cara, I know this is short notice, but..."

Delete. Delete. Delete.

"Hey Jenna! Sorry if this isn't a great time, only I..."

Delete Delete. Delete..

"Evening, Alicia! Sorry to bother you this close to dinner, but I was wondering if I could..."

Delete.

Elodie heaved a sigh of resignation and put her phone back in her bag. She was going to have to handle this on her own. She was big enough and strong enough to get herself into this mess; she should be big enough and strong enough to get herself out. But it wasn't going to be easy. And it wasn't going to be pleasant.

And it was going to require whiskey.

•　　•　　•　　•

The drive to Damian's house entailed approximately thirty minutes of nervous off-key singing along with the radio, punctuated with fraught silences as Novella tried to keep a studious eye on the rearview mirror without driving off the road. She didn't really believe James would follow her, but given her destination she couldn't take the risk. She lapped Damian's suburb twice and was aggressive with the traffic lights, rushing to make every orange that presented itself in the hope that the red would leave behind any possible tail.

Finally, she pulled into Damian's driveway and drove up past the house to where one of the garage doors was open, revealing an empty space. She wasn't totally sure that parking in his garage was acceptable but she didn't want her car visible. Something inside her felt exposed. She pondered what would happen if his wife returned to find Novella's car in her spot. While she didn't welcome a confrontation, her infatuation with Damian was such that she fully intended to stand her ground.

She looked around for a button to close the garage door, but couldn't find one. The garage was cluttered with sporting equipment and superfluous home wares that she wasn't able to step over comfortably in her purple dress with the pencil skirt, so she gave up, assuming they only had remote controls in the vehicles themselves. The garage didn't face out onto the street anyway, she reasoned, and the sensor lights only activated once you were well up the driveway. James didn't even know who Damian was, let alone where he lived. Feeling watched and uncertain, she dragged her suitcase around to the front door and rang the doorbell.

•   •   •   •

James continued to pace, back and forth, in his living room. All the information he had from the evening was collected, but unsorted in his head. He couldn't dwell on Novella suggesting they separate. The thought of losing her was so intensely painful and it didn't have to be, just yet. She was going to take some time to cool down, and then they were going to talk about it.

James felt himself coming apart at the thought of losing her. He ran his fingers through his hair roughly and sat down on the couch. He was certain he could talk her round. He just had to get through tonight, and then he wouldn't be so preoccupied. They'd been married for four years. Four wonderful years. There was still hope for them; she just needed some space. His eyes were teary and he blinked away the blur.

He stood up and began pacing again.

Dwelling on Elodie, though. That was easy. That was all he'd been doing for weeks and weeks. Months? A long time, certainly.

Elodie was the cause of so much pain; she needed to be stopped. She was bigger, these past few days. So much bigger in his head. Sometimes, it seemed as though she took up his whole body. He was aching to purge her, but she was so entwined he felt barely able to stretch his limbs without the sharp pain of her pull.

Once she was dead, all this pain would go away. And he could stop wasting all of this time on her, time he should be spending with Novella. If only he'd been able to hit her with his car that day, all of this could've been avoided. He mulled this concept over for a while, massaging it and watching it change form into the added justification he needed for tonight's plan. If Elodie had died, James wouldn't have had to neglect Novella, and Novella wouldn't be trying to leave him. He screwed up his face at the thought. Such familiar pain.

Elodie took his sister, and now she was trying to take his wife.

Filled with impetus and purpose, James set about gathering up everything on his list. He retrieved his dirty old Adidas gym bag from the boot of his car and put the solid items in first, the doorstops, the pulleys, the extra fuel. He worked with frenetic energy, checking off everything on his list as he went. The Molotov cocktails had to be wrapped carefully and stood as upright as possible. With shaking hands, he wedged them gently between the other items and carried the bag out to the car as attentively as if it contained a newborn baby.

• • • •

Damian opened the door before the doorbell had even finished its jingle. His smile was wide, but his body language remained cautious; he helped her with her suitcase, but his gaze went over her head, checking for meddlesome faces in the windows of the neighboring houses. As soon as he closed the door behind her, the façade fell away and they embraced with relief. "God, I'm so happy you're here." He spoke into her hair as he held her.

"I was so happy to get your text." Novella sighed into his shirt, exhausted from the stress of the day and relieved to finally be in his arms. "It was perfect timing. I had literally just got through the worst of it with James and was about to go pack a bag when I saw my phone light up." She grabbed his face and kissed him, and then they stood in their nervousness for a few moments, each feeling the other's anxiety and trying to convey reassurance without words.

"Did it go okay? Are you okay?" He reached inside her jacket to put his arms around her waist and hold her against him.

She let herself be enfolded by him, feeling the warmth and concern. "It went as expected. It definitely wasn't pleasant, but it's done." She stood up on tiptoes to meet his eyes. "How was your wife?"

"Yeah, it wasn't a good scene." His face fell, remembering. "But it's for the best. She needs a lot more help than I can provide." He stroked Novella's hair and gazed at her. "Would you like a glass of wine?"

"I'd love one." Novella stepped over to the wine rack that he pointed out and cast her eye over the many different colored bottles, searching for a Pinot Noir. She pulled out something sporting an award label and held it up with a questioning expression. He took it from her and carried it into the kitchen where he retrieved two beautiful, but gigantic red wine glasses.

"Wow," said Novella. "You could get a whole bottle into each of those."

"Do you want this one to yourself?" he asked.

"Oh, God no. Remember what happened last time I drank that much?"

"Of course, I remember. That was the best plan I think I've ever concocted," he said with a little smile.

This was the first Novella had heard about intention and she was both bemused and intensely flattered to discover there was pre-meditation involved. "You didn't plan that. You couldn't have known how that would go." She took a large sip of wine without taking her eyes off him.

"I knew how I hoped it would go," he said, grinning. "I already told you. I knew the moment I saw you outside my office that I was in trouble. It was only a matter of time." He came around the kitchen island to where she was perched on a barstool, looking giddy and glowing. "You need to be higher," he said, lifting her off the stool and sitting her up on the counter top so that she was at eye level. He slid his hands down to her waist and held her firmly as he kissed her. She loved the way his grasp of her was always so deliberate and secure. He trailed kisses over her check, under her jaw and down her neck. "Are you hungry?" he asked quietly.

"Starving."

"What would you like?" He was unzipping the back of her dress and sliding the straps down off her shoulders.

"To be taken to the bedroom." She smiled.

"Right answer." He bent forward and tipped her over his right shoulder. She squealed as he turned and began striding with some urgency toward the hall, his right arm thrown across the back of her knees and his left hand pulling off her heels and flinging them in various directions as he went.

CHAPTER THIRTEEN

Mental Health Services cars weren't marked, in case mentally ill people who didn't like the way they'd been treated happened upon one in an unsupervised parking lot, or worse – outside the employee's home. So, it wasn't surprising that James didn't pay any attention to the white Hyundai sedan that had pulled up across the street from his house, as he reversed out into the road.

Alister Kipp's gaze moved between his notes and the dark-haired man easing carefully down the driveway of the address he'd been given, as he realized his assignment was leaving. He wondered about getting out of the car and running out to stop him, but he didn't have a lot of information about the assignment beyond 'is agitated' and Alister didn't want to risk getting run over if the guy panicked. He made a split-second decision to follow him.

Putting the car back in gear, he pulled away from the curb and stayed reasonably close. He didn't think James would suspect a tail, since Alister had been advised he was playing an 'anonymous' call. They drove through the city and headed north. Sensing he was going somewhere specific, Alister punched a button on his phone and said loudly, "Call dispatch." The phone beeped and dialed, and a few seconds later Colleen's voice boomed through his car speakers. "Jesus Christ," he snapped, clawing at the volume button.

"Yeah, it's Alister. I went to the address Jensen requested, but the guy was leaving. I hadn't exited the vehicle yet so I'm in pursuit. I assumed Jensen would want to know."

Colleen sounded bored. "Probably. Hold on. I'll connect you."

Alister noted that James was speeding to make orange lights. He couldn't tell if he was just an aggressive driver, excited to get to the destination, or if he sensed he had a tail. He tried to keep close to James while he waited for Jensen to pick up his phone.

"You with him?" Jensen always got straight to the point.

"No, he was leaving when I arrived. I didn't get a chance to flag him down. I'm in the car now, in pursuit. He's kind of rushing. We've sprinted for two orange lights now. Heading north."

"Stay on him," Jensen replied. "And as soon as you have an address, let me know. Don't get out of the car; I did a little digging and it looks like he has an assault conviction. I'll take over when I get there."

"Roger." Alister hung up the phone and sped up to make another orange light.

•　　•　　•　　•

Elodie sat at the end of the bar in Maggie's Brasserie, nursing a whiskey on the rocks and a headache from crying. It was going to be a few more drinks before she could face going to her mother's. Just picturing it made Elodie gulp the drink in front of her and immediately wave for another.

"Jesus." Said an equally pathetic looking male in a quilted vest further down the bar, admiring her smeared mascara, puffy face, and enthusiastic drink consumption. "Bad day for you, too?"

"What gave it away?" asked Elodie dryly, responding out of habit, but not particularly wanting to engage.

"You drank that like someone else is payin' for it," said her new friend, rolling a cigarette. He had dirty blonde hair and soft eyes.

Elodie chortled. "Well, technically, someone else is." She waved her credit card. "And I don't think he'll be pleased about it, if I'm perfectly honest." She took a big swig of the freshly poured double, and then pointed at herself. "Elodie," she said, out of politeness and a false sense of obligation.

"Dwayne," he said, also pointing.

She held her glass up to him, before taking another big mouthful. "I paid extra for the top shelf," she explained, "so it tastes like honey and battery acid, instead of just battery acid."

He laughed. "I did wonder about the facial expressions you were pulling as it went down. You don't look like a whiskey-on-the-rocks kinda girl."

"Doesn't matter." She shook her head. "It's a whiskey-on-the-rocks kinda night."

He nodded slowly. "Been there."

They sat in silence for a while. Dwayne finished rolling enough cigarettes to fill his tobacco pouch and asked her if she smoked. Elodie shook her head, and he left to go outside on his own.

Alone with her thoughts, she replayed the evening with Damian. Her memory faithfully delivered a full photo album of the entire disaster, and Elodie cringed as she remembered the wine glass, and the mail, and Damian restraining her.

She didn't know what had happened. She never meant to tell Damian about Isabelle. But something about his demeanor, something about the way he wouldn't engage with her... She'd never felt so unheard, so invisible. She remembered the all-consuming rage she felt when she hurled the wine glass at the wall. It was as consistent and subconscious as her heartbeat.

She had no idea how to control it, and that was utterly humiliating because, deep down, she knew it wasn't real. It wasn't legitimate, valid rage. It was petulance. She was reacting to not getting the response she wanted. She rested her head in her hands, the hopelessness of feeling so easily manipulated permeating her entire nervous system.

A memory of Dr. Goulding resurfaced. "When we are irked by things, it is because our ego recognizes them as something we ourselves do," he'd said. Elodie blinked slowly. Was she manipulative? Certainly, her emotions elicited the desired response, but she didn't feel badly, *act* badly, in order to force Damian to react, did she? She'd always thought of it as separate to herself, a plague upon her senses that she suffered from, rather than created. But now she wondered if something deep down knew the reaction and attention was what she needed, and the tantrums were simply a method of achieving that goal.

The whiskey wasn't doing as much as she'd hoped.

She waved for another.

•   •   •   •

James drove slowly across town to Elodie's house. His lack of speed and the delicate way he rounded each corner were indicative of the care he was bestowing on the Molotov cocktails that were in his equipment bag, set snugly on the floor behind his seat. He couldn't risk them breaking or tipping over before he got to his destination. Today felt like the second most important day of his life, after his wedding day.

He smiled at the thought of Novella, pictured winning her back after Elodie was out of their lives, as he sang along to the radio and tapped frenetically on the steering wheel and the gear stick, his body desperately trying to burn off cortisol despite his stationary position. He still felt the pain of her words, but he understood where she was coming from. He had neglected her, and while it would take some time to forgive her for the affair, he truly believed with time, and possibly some therapy, they could get through it.

Besides, Novella wasn't really the one to blame. The person at the center of all this was Elodie. Novella was beautiful, and kind, and loving, and sexy, and it was perfectly understandable that someone as desirable as her would attract attention. James' mistake was making her feel like she needed to look outside their marriage for validation.

She'd made a mistake, but we all make mistakes. And he still loved her as much as the day they married. He thought back to the night of the red satin lingerie and experienced a wave of affection and gratitude for her rush through his body. Nodding along to the radio, he was excited about their life together once Elodie was dead. Once that poisonous bitch wasn't taking all his attention, he could devote himself to his and Novella's relationship.

He pictured Novella and himself on holiday on a tropical island, frolicking in the water, and making love on the sand. He wondered if she might even want to revisit the discussion about children. Everything was going to be so wonderful. He couldn't wait until all of this was sorted and he was back at home with her. He smiled at the thought as he turned up onto the freeway, the glass bottles clinking merrily in the back of the car as he merged into the flow of traffic.

•   •   •   •

Elodie was four doubles deep and feeling slightly more social by the time Dwayne came back inside from his cigarette.

"What'd I miss?" he asked.

"Uhm…" Elodie thought out loud, looking up at the ceiling, her eyes still red. "Me sniffling and self-pitying mostly. And I think someone got sick in the bathrooms behind me because they ran in really fast, and when they came out they looked really guilty and went straight out that door."

"Jesus, it all happens the minute I leave, huh." Dwayne said with a bemused expression. "So, what's the plan, Mary-Ann?"

"The plan, Stan, is I have to go home." She sighed heavily. "I have to apologize to my long-suffering husband for having a tantrum and throwing shit all over the lounge." She took a sip of her whiskey and ate one of the ice cubes with it, crunching thoughtfully as she decided whether to elaborate. "I'm going to ask him if he wants to come to therapy with me." Suddenly she laughed. "When I find a new therapist, that is. The last one binned me." She ate another ice cube.

"Can they do that?" asked Dwayne, visibly surprised.

"That's what he said!" Elodie squeaked at the déjà vu, spitting bits of splintered ice cube on the bar. She pulled a face and brushed them off onto the floor. "Must not be common. You gotta be really fucking hopeless to have someone actually turn down the money I was paying. Well, *he* was paying," she corrected herself, looking forlorn. "Anyway, I gotta go. I'm supposed to be going to my mother's, but fuck that." Dwayne watched as she slid down off her barstool, holding onto the bar as she went.

Elodie frowned. "She's a condescending bitch, and she likes my husband more than me. More than she likes me, I mean. Not more than I like my husband. I really like him. I love him." She looked earnestly at Dwayne. "I love him so much." Her voice broke. "I need to go tell him I'm sorry right now. I hit him. I can't believe I hit him," she said into her handbag as she rummaged around for her keys.

"You're not driving, are you?" asked Dwayne.

Elodie rushed to think of an excuse so he wouldn't attempt to stop her. She dropped the keys back into the bag. "No, of course not! I'm just looking for my phone. My friend's picking me up." She slung her bag over her shoulder and teetered past him to the door. "Nice to meet you. See you next time."

Dwayne turned to see her reach the door, grab the handle, and lean on it with all her body weight. She could feel his eyes on her as she took a moment to register her own confusion, then pull the door open and walk outside into the cool night air.

• • • •

James had to keep stopping himself from humming as he went about his preparations. As summer was coming to a close, some of the trees on Elodie's street had begun to turn a beautiful golden brown, like perfectly cooked pancakes, and he took a moment to lament that this adventure had to happen in the dark without the beautiful background of such glorious scenery. While the days were still beach-worthy, the nights had transitioned from balmy to crisp, and there were a few dog walkers out, grateful that the cloying humidity had finally eased.

James, too, was pleased that the night air was light and cool, as he had dressed all in black for the evening's events and he needed the anonymity of his hooded sweater. He gently eased the gym bag out of the foot well and rested it on the back seat. He put two elastic pulleys and a hand towel over his shoulder, tucked a couple of wooden wedges under his arm, and lifted both petrol bombs out of the bag.

He took a moment to inspect and adjust the rags he'd stuffed in the top, making sure they weren't too sodden, and tucked a few stray bits of fabric back into place. They were lovingly wrapped in brown paper bags in case he was approached as he strolled up to the house. He didn't mind being confused with a drunk or a dinner guest, as long as no one got in his way.

He looked around the neighborhood, gently lit by the unobstructed glow of the full moon. The beautiful homes with the manicured lawns stoked the flames of his anger and energized his approach. Somewhere deep in his subconscious he had always associated money with dishonesty, and so the opportunity to punish Elodie and simultaneously vandalize such a nice neighborhood was both welcome and exhilarating.

The smell of the petrol was, in a strange way, appetizing, and a taste of things to come. He looked forward to consuming and reliving the heat and the memories for the last time. The part of him that found solace and catharsis in the flames was yearning for the savory scent of smoke and the homely crackle of the fire engulfing its prey. After the last dog walker had passed, he closed the car door and walked briskly up the sidewalk towards the house.

•   •   •   •

"Do you think you'll keep this place?" asked Novella, stroking Damian's back as he lay across her, deep in the afterglow.

"Mm, not sure," he replied, sleepily. One of his arms was still under her back from where he'd been holding on to her so tightly a moment ago, and the warmth emanating from his palm was a delectable contrast to the cool night air flowing in through the partially-open bedroom window behind her. It reminded her of being in a hot jacuzzi outside at a ski resort. She was content.

She stroked his hair and kissed his head. He smiled and murmured something about making her some dinner. "Don't move just yet," she said quickly. "I'm loving the warmth and weight of you."

"Are you insinuating that I'm heavy?" He grinned, lifting his head to kiss along her collarbone.

"In the best possible way," she replied, pulling his free arm up over her as though he were a blanket. When he got to the end of her collarbone he bit her shoulder. She breathed in sharply and he turned her face towards him so that he could kiss her. She arched against him and kicked the sheet away so she could embrace him with her whole body. "It's a good thing you like me on top of you," he said, playfully, "because we might be here a while"

He reached over the side of the bed and picked his tie and belt up off the floor. Her eyes widened. He sat back on his knees, grabbed her by the wrist and pulled her arm up so that he could secure it to the bed post. She watched him, mesmerized, as he moved around her and fixed the other wrist to the bed with such dexterity that she was immediately certain he'd done this before. Once she was properly restrained, he took a moment to admire the view, before climbing back onto the bed and lowering his head to her breasts.

•　　•　　•　　•

Outside the bar, Elodie rummaged around in her handbag for her keys. She wobbled across the parking lot to where her black BMW sat, thankfully reverse parked, but taking up two spaces.

"Oops." She giggled to herself, eventually locating the keys and immediately dropping them onto the gravel. "Fuck's sake."

She managed to put a decent scratch in the door, missing the lock badly and having to press her left hand against the window of the car to steady herself enough to find the little silver slot. She cursed herself for not replacing the battery in the fob. It had died fairly recently and she meant to get it replaced after coffee with her mother, but after their tense and unpleasant discussion, she was too caught up in what she was supposed to be doing to keep Damian. She laughed at the irony as she sat down heavily in the driver's seat.

After a few fruitless tries, she managed to get the key in the ignition. With the engine running, she adjusted the air conditioning and flipped open the visor mirror to check her eye makeup. "Shit!" she lamented, pulling tissues out of the center console and wiping away more mascara streaks. She reached into her handbag for her makeup compact and added a little more eyeliner. She blinked a few times to try and establish whether both eyes were finished and even, but she couldn't focus for that level of detail. It would have to do.

She put the visor up and depressed the clutch. First gear was always sticky and took a couple of pushes. Thanks to her platform heels, she misjudged how far out her foot was and stalled the car. It jumped and died, giving her a fright. She let out a huge sigh and blinked furiously, swallowing back tears.

She reached down and pulled her heels off, flinging them haphazardly at the passenger's side, then put the clutch back in, barefooted, and started the car again.

CHAPTER FOURTEEN

James had adopted a purposeful stride on his way to burn targets for two reasons. Mainly because confidence gave people the impression that you were supposed to be there, lessening the chance that they'd call the police on you, but also because he needed his physiology to support his mission. He couldn't creep up to the sprawling house nervously, with his hands shaking and his mind trying to talk him out of it. What if the bombs didn't break? What if the target was off? No. He had a plan. And the plan was Elodie goes up in flames. That's how it was going to be. He was ready, he was prepared, and he wasn't risking another close call.

He could see through the front windows that no one was in the lounge or kitchen, but there were lights on throughout the house, so he was confident she was home. The soft frosted lighting made the lounge look staged, like it was ready for a magazine photo-shoot. He pictured the scene on the cover of *Better Homes and Gardens* and smirked.

He moved quickly and silently along the shrub lining of the driveway until he could cross over to the front door. In fact, there were two front doors. Heavy oak beauties with ornate, elongated handles in gypsy gold that swung outward in a welcoming French style. Setting the Molotov cocktails down carefully on the porch, he took one of the wooden doorstops out from under his arm, pressed the thin edge into the tiny gap at the bottom of the door, and gave it a short shove with his hand.

Confident that it was in place, he stood, turned sideways and gave it a sharp kick with the heel of his shoe to make sure it was properly wedged underneath. He did the same to the other door, though the tell-tale cobwebs along the hinge-side and across the top told him that they rarely used that side. It may even be jammed shut, he mused, noting the dusting of rust over the hinge screws and the rainwater staining underneath it. He wore a small smile as he pictured Elodie pushing frantically on the doors, coughing through the smoke, her eyes streaming.

He moved away from the door without making a sound, and peered up around to the glass paneling at the front to see if he'd disturbed anyone. He stood, unmoving against the side of the house. His black clothes helped him blend into the odd shapes and shadows thrown against the cladding by the various statues and outdoor furniture as he waited, listening intently for footsteps or voices. Hearing nothing, he stepped down off the porch and walked along the side of the house, looking for the back door.

He found it, at the rear of the house on the right-hand side. The entire back section was set up for outdoor entertaining, with an expansive verandah that continued up the side of the house, stopping at the fence dividing the front and back yards. James came up the steps slowly, praying there weren't any loose, squeaky boards, and took the pulleys off his shoulder.

He linked them together and connected the verandah railing to the door, so that they wouldn't be able to pull the door open. He had to put his bodyweight behind it to get the elastic to loop around the rail and hook onto itself again, but he managed to get it strung tight without grunting too loudly. Confident that no one was getting out either door, he went in search of whatever bedroom or bathroom Elodie was in.

The verandah wasn't the quietest structure to walk on, but as it hugged the entire back half of the house, James had to stay on it if he wanted to have access to the rooms whose windows looked out over the expansive back yard. The beautifully landscaped area was full of bold, fruitful apple trees and bushes of bright purple beautyberries, their deep violet tint only visible in parts of the tree able to catch a glimmer of light from the house.

James rounded the corner of the house and was greeted with his holy grail. A few meters ahead, he spied a large window, partially open, with the bottom half frosted for privacy. His heart rate increased at the sight of the finish line. As he peered in, he could see a mirror atop a tallboy against the interior wall, confirming for him that it was indeed a bedroom, and he was just about to sprint up, reach through the window, and slam the petrol bomb down when he was struck by a thought.

Bedrooms were carpeted.

What if the bottle didn't break? He looked down at the vessel he'd chosen. The base was quite thick. He crouched down again, pausing the plan while he racked his brain for an answer. He looked at the window. It was hinged at the top and open about forty-five degrees. Suddenly he had an idea. He would throw the bomb *up*.

He would throw it upwards with all his might and have it shatter on the ceiling, raining flaming petrol down over the whole room and, with a bit of luck, everyone in it. For a second, James thought he heard a man's voice through the open window, but all sound was mostly static over the dull roar of his own pulse in his ears.

The mental image of Elodie being doused in flaming petrol flashed in his mind and he was momentarily excited, before the memories were interspersed with pictures of Isabelle screaming in flames. James tried to follow both movies in his head at the same time and the effort knotted his forehead together. He ached from the tension and the anguish. He put his head in his hands and pressed hard on his temples, his eyes screwed shut. He breathed heavily through his nose. "Elodie. Elodie," he whispered to himself, trying to focus on her face alone.

He stood up slowly and flexed his legs from where they'd stiffened in the crouch, leaving one bomb alone on the verandah. He stepped silently up to the window, hugging the edge of the house. At the edge of the window frame, he reached into his pocket for a lighter. Before lighting the fuse, he put one foot in front of the other, trying to find a comfortable stance from which to throw. He felt the weight of the bomb a few times, and took a few 'practice swings' to make sure he had the trajectory just right.

Confident that he was ready to throw, he lit the fuse. It caught easily and he resumed the stance. Bending at the knees, he focused upwards on the part of the ceiling he was aiming for, and on the silent count of three, hurled the bomb straight up through the window with everything he had.

As expected, the bottle hit the ceiling at a reasonable speed and shattered, sending hyper-oxygenated petrol half-spraying, half-raining down all over the bedroom. The room lit up like a fireworks display. He could tell from the light and the smoke that the bed linen was alight almost immediately, and the shocked screaming told him his target was in the room. He was momentarily ecstatic but couldn't rest on his laurels; she would no doubt run out of the bedroom – he needed to get to the other end of the house.

No longer worried about security lights, he sprinted down the side of the house and through the gate in the dividing fence. Through the glass panels at the front, he could see floor length curtains and magazines and papers all over the floor. His target selected, he needed a way in. Snatching the hand towel off his shoulder, he wrapped it around the middle of his arm clumsily and stomped through the garden to get to the glass. Turning his head away he elbowed himself a decent sized hole, and used the towel to push out a couple of remaining shards.

He took his lighter out again, lit the second fuse, reached through and launched the last bomb as hard as he could against the far wall, closest to the sheer curtains. A waterfall of orange lit up the entire north end of the living space, devouring the curtains and pouncing on the junk mail and magazines so considerately strewn across the floor. Each item provided the fire a stepping stone to the most flammable pieces of furniture, ensuring the room was well ablaze in barely a few minutes. James let out a breathy laugh, relieved and elated. He hugged his arms around his ribcage, suffused with joy.

•　　•　　•　　•

Elodie was feeling quite drunk and a little vulnerable behind the wheel. She knew she shouldn't be driving, but absolutely had to get to Damian. She didn't expect him to welcome her back with open arms, but she needed to apologize. They couldn't leave things like this. And if she was able to get some kind of agreement from him that therapy (or at the very least, discussion) was still on the cards, then she could go to her mother's, not entirely devoid of hope.

The thought of what her mother would say made her feel physically ill, which she couldn't handle on top of all the neat whiskey sloshing around in her stomach. So, she sang along to the radio, in key, but out of time, as she drove, stopping dutifully at every orange light for fear of attracting attention. Stopped at the last set of lights before home, she blew her nose and checked herself in the mirror one last time before turning into her street.

•　　•　　•　　•

The skin on Novella's arm was blistering as she screamed in horror at the inferno unfolding around her. The flames whipped across the fabric of the polyester tie that bound her as she kicked and bucked, frantically trying to wrench her arm away from the intense heat. Damian swatted at the tie, trying to pat down the flames so he could access the knot, but the spilled petrol was prolonging the burn and he couldn't get his fingers onto the cloth as she squirmed and yelped through the pain.

Terrified, he gave up and rushed to her other side to unclip the leather belt around her right wrist. Partially freed, she scrambled up onto her knees and yanked with all her might, tearing through the leftover polyester. The stringy fabric slid through her freshly melted skin and she howled and cradled the scorched and weeping limb like a baby bird.

They stumbled towards the bedroom door, Damian trying to outrun the heat he felt on his back, the splatters of petrol accented with motor oil burning into his skin and emitting a sickening smell. She could hear his ragged breathing as he fled to the back door, turned the handle and pulled. It didn't open. Panicked, he jerked it back and forth with all his strength, but it wouldn't move. He turned and bolted down the hallway. Novella struggled to change direction quickly as the pain of moving her arm around blanketed her mind. Over her whimpering, she heard him shout, "There's an extinguisher in the kitchen!" before dissolving into a coughing fit.

"Get down!" she shrieked back, dropping to her knees to find cleaner air as the clouds of filthy black smoke billowed above them.

They crawled into the kitchen and Damian dived at the cabinets under the sink. Pulling the door open roughly, he was horrified to see the mounting bracket empty. Novella registered devastation on his face as he realized that he'd had it outside during their last barbeque, and the extinguisher was likely still in the garage.

Novella was in the fetal position, cosseting her charred arm, caked in partially clotted blood, and coughing through her sobs of agony.

"Get up!" Damian rasped at her with his last full breath of air.

Keeping their heads low to the ground, they staggered to the front door where he again turned the door handle and shoved with no success. "FUCK!?" he screamed, ramming his shoulder against it twice, three times. He tried the other one, with the same outcome, before sliding to the floor, too depleted of oxygen to carry himself any longer. He looked to the glass windows in desperation.

Novella was on her knees heaving and whimpering next to him. He reached out to touch her shoulder to tell her that they needed to get to the windows, but his vision blurred and his muscles began to relax. He collapsed next to her, each of them gasping and struggling to remain conscious. She extended her arm and rested her hand on his face just as everything went black.

•　　•　　•　　•

Detective Jensen skidded to a halt about fifty yards behind the crowd of neighbors and leapt out of his car. He sprinted up to where Alister was standing at the front of the crowd and grabbed him roughly by the back of his sweater. "Where is he?!"

Alister jumped, taking a moment to register who was yelling at him. "I... I'm not sure. Probably round the back of the house?"

"Why didn't you stop him?!"

"You told me not to get out of the car! I thought you were on your way. Did you come via Mexico?!"

"Jesus Christ, what happened? Did anyone call the fire service?"

"Of course." Sensing the bystanders beginning to crowd around, they jogged out of the throng to continue talking. "I called them as soon as I heard screaming. I didn't know what he was doing. It looked like he was just creeping around the house. Is he a stalker?"

Jensen looked up at the house, defeated. "He's an arsonist."

•　　•　　•　　•

The fire was breathtaking and James was high. From the side of the house, he could enjoy the smell of the smoke, acrid and dense from the motor oil he'd so spitefully added, and the sight of the giant flames hungrily devouring the inside of the house. It was so therapeutic. Giant waves of orange danced around the building, crackling and cozy. Everything James had envisioned and more. In his joyful haze, he tried to watch the spectacle for a little longer as he made his way towards his car.

He came around to the left side of the house, keeping to the shadows. Across the driveway and further down, he could see the double garage. The left door was up and there was a dark car inside. He expected it to be a black BMW, but it wasn't. James slowed down and tipped his head to the side, processing. He hadn't thought about Elodie having a partner, though he was resigned to the possibility of someone else being in the house with her when she died. His mind flashed back to the moment on the verandah before he threw the first bomb, when he thought he heard a male voice. Sad, he thought, enjoying the heat on his back. His serene smile faded as his eyes caught sight of the license plate.

N0VE11A

A creeping cold slipped over his shoulders, enveloping his chest. He spun around to face the house, a scream building in the back of his throat. The inside of the house was completely engulfed, and several of the back windows had already blown out. The rising panic smashed through his morbid celebration and he leapt from foot to foot, trying to figure out where to go in the confusion of his realization. The panic up under his sternum felt like it was gathering up his lungs with icy fingers. He struggled to breathe as he used what little oxygen he could muster to cry.

•   •   •   •

Elodie had slowed as she approached her block. Her heart sank as she saw the police cruiser. The street was clogged with dozens of her neighbors outside on their front lawns in various degrees of night wear, watching her house collapse under the weight of the biggest fire most of them had ever seen. The whiskey glow was yanked off her like a needle from a record and she swerved around them to get to her driveway, frantically hitting the horn.

Elodie careened over the curb, popped the car out of gear and slammed on the brakes, leaving deep tire marks in the soft grass in front of her fence.

"DAMIAN!"

Her shrill cry sped across the night air and the neighbors looked at each other in shock. The engine was still running as she leapt from the driver's seat, trying to see a way in.

• • • •

James was on his knees by the garage. He stood up when Elodie came flying into the front yard, squinting at her with anguished recognition as she shrieked a man's name over and over again.

Her husband was in there?

With James' wife.

James doubled over as the icy fingers scrunched his lungs again. The world was spinning and he needed to vomit, but his empty stomach had nothing to offer. He retched a few times, letting out guttural sobs in between. He'd wanted so much to destroy her, and he'd destroyed both of them in the process. Revenge was anything but sweet.

Elodie danced back and forth in front of the house for a little while as though she thought she could get inside. James caught sight of her blurry outline just as she launched herself in the direction of the front door. "NO!" he yelled, instinctively sprinting forward and looping an arm around her waist to pull her back from the house.

Elodie kicked and struggled against him, a waterfall of tears streaming freely down her face as she gazed at her demolished house. "Let me go! LET ME GO!"

"It's too late!" James yelled in her ear. "They're gone." He choked on the last word. His knees gave out and he pulled her down with him onto the lawn. He didn't loosen his grip in case she made another run for it. She sobbed harder for his words, clawing his sweater and howling.

•　•　•　•

Elodie was hyperventilating. James put his arms around her and hugged her to him to try and calm her down enough to breathe. With her face against his sweater she took her first proper gulp of air, and instantly recognized the heady, aromatic scent of petrol. She pushed back from him in shock. Realizing who he was, her hands came to her face in shock.

She scrambled backwards away from him, holding his gaze until she was sure he wasn't coming after her. The main front window exploded outward, making the whole neighborhood cry out in fright and showering the front yard with broken glass. The wail of sirens was audible in the distance. The front wall began to sag and hung precariously, threatening to take the entire front half of the roof with it. Elodie sobbed louder, staring at her burning house.

"I'm so sorry!" she cried, desperate to deliver the apology she had planned so sincerely. "I'm so sorry, Damian."

CHAPTER FIFTEEN

James' grief had anesthetized him against the heat and the glass, a piece of which had embedded itself just above his collar bone. He reached up and pulled it out, smearing the blood that was running down his chest and soaking his t-shirt. He looked back at Elodie, screaming her apologies over and over again on the lawn, the dancing light of the blaze highlighting the floods of tears that continued down her face.

James recognized Detective Jensen as he approached, carrying a pair of handcuffs. There was another man with him that James hadn't seen before, carrying some kind of blanket. The stranger made a beeline for Elodie, keeping a nervous-looking eye on James as he went. He didn't look like a police officer.

James didn't move. He was thinking about the other fires. He had needed those to get through the days, and so he had felt justified in taking them. But now, with Novella gone, nothing else seemed to matter. Tidal waves of loss and regret washed over him as he stood, swaying slightly, watching the house disintegrate and cremate his beautiful wife.

•   •   •   •

Alister interrupted Elodie's sermon of atonement with a quiet greeting. She sat up slowly, slivers of glass dangling from her hair and jacket, sparkling like diamonds in the light of the flames. She looked over at James. His face was smeared with blood and tears and underneath his left eye was twitching. Elodie inched across the lawn on all fours with Alister following behind, pushing chunks of glass away to make spaces to rest her knees as she went. She stopped when she saw the detective grab James by the wrist and place the first cuff on him.

"Hey!" she said, still shaking from the adrenaline. James locked eyes with her as Jensen grabbed his other wrist and secured his hands together behind his back. He winced through a small smile.

"Come on." Detective Jensen held James' upper arm and tried to steer him away from the house. The heat was intense and he was sweating profusely. "No," said James, wrenching his arm away sharply and taking off in the other direction.

"NO!" Elodie shrieked. She tried to leap up after him, but Alister locked her in an embrace, padded by the blanket he was carrying. In the distance, several of the neighbors screamed as James' outline blurred on entry into the fire. The front of the house finally collapsed, the flaming roof completely engulfing the verandah, sending a mushroom cloud of smoke and sparks up into the night sky.

THE END

AUTHOR BIO

Sarah Reilly is a Life Coach by day and fiction writer by night. An avid traveller, she wrote this book in Indonesia, edited it in England and published it in Canada. You can get in touch with her at SarahReillyCoaching.com or on most social media channels.

Printed in Australia
AUHW010938151019
318599AU00001B/4